McKenna pulled back.

But Desmond still had her trapped between his body and the table. Her pulse thundered in her ears as they stared at each other.

"That was…"

"Amazing?" he supplied, his gaze hot. "Yeah. But I'm sensing we're going to stop now."

"See, we communicate just fine." She gulped. "I'm just…not sure this is a good idea."

They were not two people who had the luxury of an uncomplicated fling. They were married with a divorce agreement already hammered out. That was not a recipe for experimentation, and she wasn't much of an experimenter anyway.

Where could this possibly go?

"Oh, it's a good idea." His piercing gaze tore her open inside as he promised her exactly how good it would be without saying a word. "But we both have to think so."

With that, he stepped back, releasing her.

She took a deep breath and nodded. He was being gentlemanly about it, putting all the balls in her court. "I agree. And I don't think that right now."

Her mind didn't, at least. Even if her body did.

* * *

The Marriage Contract
is part of Mills & Boon Desire's Nº1 bestselling series,
Billionaires and Babies: Powerful men…
wrapped around their babies' little fingers.

THE MARRIAGE CONTRACT

BY
KAT CANTRELL

First Published in Great Britain 2017
By Mills & Boon, an imprint of HarperCollins*Publishers*
1 London Bridge Street, London, SE1 9GF

© 2017 Kat Cantrell

ISBN: 978-0-263-06901-3

Our policy is to use papers that are natural, renewable and recyclable
products and made from wood grown in sustainable forests. The logging
and manufacturing processes conform to the legal environmental
regulations of the country of origin.

Printed and bound in Great Britain
by CPI Antony Rowe, Chippenham, Wiltshire

USA TODAY bestselling author **Kat Cantrell** read her first Mills & Boon novel in third grade and has been scribbling in notebooks since she learned to spell. She's a Harlequin So You Think You Can Write winner and a Romance Writers of America Golden Heart® Award finalist. Kat, her husband and their two boys live in north Texas.

Dayna Hart: this one is for you
because *Beauty and the Beast* is your favorite.

One

Despite never having believed in miracles, Desmond Pierce witnessed one at 7:23 p.m. on an otherwise non-descript Tuesday as he glimpsed his son for the first time.

A nurse in navy blue scrubs carried the mewling infant into the small room off the main hospital corridor where Desmond had been instructed to wait. The moment his gaze lit on the baby, he felt a zap of recognition in his gut.

My son.

Awed into speechlessness, Des reached out to touch the future.

Warmth and something totally foreign clogged his throat. Tears. Joy. Vindication.

Amazing. Who knew money really *could* buy happiness?

The kid's face screwed up in a wail of epic proportions as if the nurse had poked him with a pin. Des felt his son's distress with deeper empathy than he'd ever experienced before—and that was saying something. It winnowed through his pores, sensitizing his muscles almost to the point of pain as he held himself back from snatching the boy from the nurse's arms.

Was this terrible combination of wonder, reverence and absolute terror what it was like for all parents? Or had he been gifted with a special bond because his son wouldn't have a mother?

"How are you this evening, Mr. Pierce?" the nurse inquired pleasantly.

"Regretting the sizable donation I made to this establishment," he growled and immediately bemoaned not taking a moment to search for a more acceptable way to communicate. This, after he'd *vowed* not to be his usual gruff self. "Why is my son crying?"

Better. More in the vein of how he'd practiced in the mirror. But the hard cross of his arms over his chest didn't quell the feeling that something was wrong. The baby hadn't been real these last forty weeks, or rather Des hadn't let himself believe that this pregnancy would end differently than Lacey's.

Now that he'd seen the baby, all the stars aligned. And there was no way in hell he'd let anything happen to his son.

"He's hungry," the nurse returned with a cautious half smile. "Would you like to feed him?"

Yes. He would. But he had to nod as emotion gripped his vocal cords.

An explosion of teddy bears climbed the walls behind the rocking chair the nurse guided him to. A vinyl-sided cabinet with a sink occupied the back corner and the counter was strewed with plastic bottles.

Des had done a lot of research into bottle-feeding, as well as all other aspects of parenting: philosophies of child rearing, behavioral books by renowned specialists, websites with tips for new parents. He'd committed a lot of it to memory easily, largely owing to his excitement and interest in the subject, but then, he held two doctorates from Harvard. There were not many academics that he hadn't mastered. He was pretty sure he could handle a small task like sticking the nipple into the baby's mouth.

Carefully she settled the baby into his arms with a gentle smile. "Here you go, Dad. It's important that you hold him as much as possible."

Des zeroed in on the pink wrinkled face and the entire world fell away. His son weighed nothing at all. Less than a ten-pound barbell. Wonder tore a hole through Desmond's chest as he held his son for the first time. Instantly he cataloged everything his senses could soak in. Dark eyes. Dark hair peeking from under the knit cap.

Conner Clark Pierce. His son.

Whatever it took, he'd move heaven and earth to give this new person everything. Private tutors, trips to educational sites like the pyramids at Giza and Machu Picchu, a workshop that rivaled his father's if he wanted to invent things like Des did. The baby would have every advantage and would never want for anything, let alone a mother.

The nurse pulled the hat down more firmly on the baby's head. That's when Conner started yowling again. The baby's anguish bled through Desmond's skin, and he did not like it.

The nurse turned to the back counter. "Let me make you a bottle."

She measured out the formula over the sound of the baby's cries, which grew more upsetting as the seconds ticked by.

Des had always felt other people's pain deeply, which

was one of the many reasons he avoided crowds, but his response to his son was so much worse than general empathy. This little person shared his DNA, and whether the suggestion of it sharpened the quickening under his skin or there really was a genetic bond, the urgency of the situation could not be overstated.

She finally crossed to Des, where he'd settled into the rocking chair, and handed him the bottle. Like he'd watched in countless videos, he held the nipple to the baby's bottom lip and tipped it.

His son's lower lip trembled as he wailed, but he would not take the bottle. Des would never describe himself as patient, but he tried diligently fourteen more times.

"Why is he refusing?" Des asked the nurse as the sense of something being wrong welled up in his chest again.

"I don't know." She banked the concern in her expression but not before Des saw it. "It's not unusual for babies who are taken from their mothers to have difficulty acclimating. We can try with a dropper. A bottle isn't the only way to get the formula into his body."

Desmond nodded and bit his tongue as the nurse crowded into his space.

The dropper worked. For about five minutes. Then Conner started spitting up all over everything. The nurse frowned again and her expression tingled his spine.

Thirty minutes later, all three of them were frustrated.

"It seems he might have an allergy to formula," the nurse finally announced.

"What does that mean? He's going to starve?" Des shut his eyes in pure agony and scrubbed at his beard, which could probably use trimming but, like usual, he'd forgotten. Sometimes Mrs. Elliot, his housekeeper, reminded him, but only if they crossed paths and, lately, he'd been hiding out in his workshop in preparation for today.

For no reason apparently, since none of his prep had covered this scenario.

"No, we're not going to let that happen. We've got some options…" She trailed off. "Never mind that one. I've been made aware of your wishes regarding your son's mother, so—"

"Forget my wishes and tell me your suggestion. The baby has to eat," Des insisted.

The nurse nodded. "The baby might breast-feed. I mean, this is highly unusual. Typically it's the other way around, where we have to supplement a mother's breast milk with formula until a lactation consultant can work with her, but—"

The baby's wails cut her off.

"She's still here? At the hospital?" He'd never met his son's surrogate mother, as they'd agreed, but he was desperate for a solution.

"Well, yes. Of course. Most women take a couple of days to recover from childbirth but—"

"Take me to her." His mind went to work on how he could have said that better, but distress wasn't the best state for a do-over. "Please."

Relief eased the nurse's expression and she nodded. "Just a warning. She might not be willing to breast-feed."

"I'll convince her," he countered as he stood with the baby in his arms.

His agreement with McKenna Moore, his son's surrogate mother, had loopholes for medical necessities. Plus, she was still legally his wife; they'd married by proxy to avoid any legal snarls, but their relationship was strictly professional. Despite the fact that they had never met, hopefully being married would count for something. The baby had to eat—as soon as Desmond convinced Conner's mother that she was his only hope.

Frankly, asking for her help was a last resort. Their agreement limited Ms. Moore's involvement with the baby because Des wanted a family that was all his own. But he was desperate to look after his son's welfare.

Out into the hall they went. At room 247, the nurse stopped and inclined her head. "Give me a second to see if she's accepting visitors."

Des nodded. The baby had quieted during the walk, which was a blessing. The rocking motion had soothed him most likely. Good information to have at his disposal.

Voices from inside the room drifted out into the hall.

"He wants to what?" The feminine lilt that did not belong to the nurse could only be McKenna Moore's. She was awake and likely decent by this time since the nurse was in the room.

The baby stirred, his little face lifting toward the sound. And that decided it. Conner recognized his mother's voice and, despite the absolute conviction that the best way to handle this surrogacy situation was to never be in the same room with the woman who had given birth to his son, Desmond pushed open the door with his foot and entered.

The dark-haired figure in the hospital bed drew his eye like a siren song and when their gazes met a jolt of recognition buzzed through all his senses at once. The same sort as when he'd glimpsed his son for the first time. *Their* son.

This woman was his child's mother. This woman was his *legally wedded wife*.

McKenna Moore's features were delicate and beautiful and he'd never been so ruthlessly stirred by someone in his life. He couldn't speak, couldn't think, and for a man with a genius IQ, lack of brain function was alarming indeed. As was the sudden, irrevocable conviction that he'd made a terrible mistake in the way he'd structured the surrogacy agreement.

He couldn't help but mourn the lost opportunity to woo this woman, to get to know her. To have the option to get her pregnant the old-fashioned way.

How in the hell had he developed such a visceral attraction to his wife in the space of a few moments?

Didn't matter. He hadn't met her first because he hated to navigate social scenarios. He stumbled over the kinds of relationships that seemed easy and normal for others, which was why he lived in a remote area of Oregon, far from Astoria, the nearest city.

Desmond had always been that weird kid at the corner table. Graduating from high school at fifteen hadn't helped him forge a lot of connections. Neither had becoming a billionaire. If he'd tried to have a normal relationship with McKenna Moore, it would have ended in disaster in the same fashion as the one he'd tried with Lacey.

Bonds of blood, like the one he shared with his son, were the only answer for someone like him. This baby would be his family and fulfill Desmond's craving for an heir. Maybe his son would even love him just because.

Regardless, the baby belonged to *him*. Desmond decided what would happen to his kid and there was no one on this entire planet who could trump his wishes.

Except for maybe his wife.

But he'd paid his law firm over a million dollars to ensure the prenuptial agreement protected his fortune and an already-drafted divorce decree granted him full custody. It was ironclad, or rather, would be as soon as he filed for the divorce.

She'd recover from childbirth, take Desmond's divorce settlement money and vanish. Exactly as he'd envisioned when he'd determined the only thing that could fill the gaping hole in his life was a baby to replace the one he'd lost—or rather, the one Lacey had aborted.

Never again would he allow a woman to dictate something as critical as to whether his child would live or die. And never again would he let himself care about a woman who held even a smidgen of power over his happiness. One day, his son would understand.

"Ms. Moore," he finally growled out long past the time when it would have been appropriate to start speaking. "We have a problem. Our son needs you."

Desmond Pierce stood in McKenna's hospital room. With a crying baby.

Her baby.

The one she'd been trying really hard to forget she'd just pushed out of her body in what had to be the world's record for painful, difficult labors…and then given away.

McKenna's eyes widened as she registered what he'd just said and her eye sockets were so dry, even that hurt. Everything hurt. She wanted codeine and to sleep for three days, not a continual spike through her heart with each new cry of the baby. The muscles in her arms tensed to reach for her son so she could touch him.

She wasn't supposed to see the baby. Or hold him. The nurse had told her that when they'd taken him away, even though McKenna had begged for the chance to say goodbye. The cruel people in the delivery room had ignored her. What did they know about sacrifice? About big, gaping holes inside that nothing would ever fill?

For a second she'd thought her son's father had figured that out. That he'd come strictly to grant her wish.
The look on his face as he'd come through the door—
it had floored her. Their gazes connected and it was as
if he could see all her angst and last-minute indecision.
And understood.

I've come to fix everything, he seemed to say without a word.

But that was not the reality of why Mr. Pierce was
here with the baby. Instead he was here to rip her heart
to shreds. Again.

They should leave. Right now. Before she started crying.

"He's not my son," she rasped, her vocal cords still
strained from the trauma of birth.

She shouldn't have said that. The phrase—both true
and brutal—unfolded inside her with sharp teeth, tearing at her just as deeply as the baby's cries.

He *was* her son. The one she'd signed away because it
ticked all the boxes in her head that her parents had lined
up. *You should find a man, have lots of babies*, they'd
said. *There's no greater joy than children.*

Except she didn't want kids. She wanted to be a doctor, to help people in pain and in need. Desmond had
yearned for a baby; she could give him one and experience pregnancy without caving in to her parent's pressure. They didn't approve of western medicine. It was
a huge source of conflict, especially after Grandfather
had died when homeopathic remedies had failed to cure
his cancer.

Being Desmond Pierce's surrogate allowed her a cre-
ative way to satisfy her parents and still contribute to so-
ciety according to what made sense to *her*. That's what
she'd repeated to herself over and over for the last hour

and she'd almost believed it—until a man had burst into her hospital room with a crying baby in his arms.

And he was looking at her so strangely that she felt compelled to prompt him. "What do you want, Desmond?"

They'd never been formally introduced, but the baby was a dead giveaway. Desmond Pierce didn't look anything like the pictures she'd searched on the internet. Of course she'd had a better-than-average dose of curiosity about the man with such strict ideas about the surrogacy arrangement, the man who would marry her without meeting her.

But this man—he made tall, dark and handsome seem banal. He was *fascinating*, with a scruff of a beard that gave him a dangerous edge, deep brown hair swept back from his face and a wiry build.

Desmond Pierce was the perfect man to be a father or she wouldn't have agreed to his proposal. What she hadn't realized was that he was a perfect man, *period*. Coupled with the baby in his arms, he might well be the most devastatingly handsome male on the planet.

And then she realized. He wasn't just a man. They were married. He was *her husband*. Whom she was never supposed to meet.

"The baby won't eat," he said over the yowls. "You need to try to breast-feed him."

She blinked. Twice. "I need to do what?"

"The nurse said he's allergic to formula. We've tried for an hour." He moved closer to the bed with a purposeful stride that brooked no nonsense and held out the wailing bundle. "He needs you. This is the one thing I cannot give him."

She stared at the wrinkled face of her child, refusing to reach out, refusing to let the wash of emotions beating through her chest take hold. The baby needed her and she was the sole person who could help. But how could she? Breast-feeding was far too nurturing of a thing to do with a baby she wasn't allowed to keep.

How dare Desmond come in here and layer on more impossible emotional turmoil in the middle of her already-chaotic heart?

She'd done her part according to their agreement. The baby was born, healthy and the child was set for life with a billionaire father who wanted him badly enough to seek out an unusual surrogacy agreement and who had the means to take care of him. What more could Desmond Pierce possibly expect from her? Did he want to slice off a piece of her soul when he took her baby away for the second time?

"That's too much to ask," she whispered even as her breasts tingled at the suggestion. They'd grown hard and heavy the moment the baby had entered the room crying. It was simple physiology and she'd known she'd have to let her milk dry up. Had been prepared for it.

What she had not been prepared for was the request to use it to feed her son.

Desmond's brows came together. "You're concerned about your figure?"

That shouldn't have been so funny. "Yeah, I'm entering the Miss USA pageant next week and how I'll look in a bikini is definitely my biggest objection."

"That's sarcasm, right?"

The fact that he had to ask struck her oddly, but before she could comment, he stuck the baby right into her arms. Against her will, her muscles shifted, cradling the baby to her bosom, and she was lost. As he must have known. As the nurse had known.

She shouldn't be holding the baby, but she was, and it

was too late to stop the thunder of her pulse as it pumped awe and love and duty and shock straight to her heart.

My son.

He still cried, his face rooting against her breast, and it was clear what he wanted. She just hadn't realized how deeply her desire to give it to him would ultimately go.

"There's a clause in the custody agreement about the baby's medical needs," Desmond reminded her. "You're on the hook for eighteen years if he needs you for medical reasons."

"Yeah, but I thought that would only be invoked if he needed a kidney or something," she blurted as the baby's little fingers worked blindly against her chest. "Not breast-feeding."

She *couldn't.* Judging by how badly she wanted to, if she did this, it would be so much harder to walk away. It wasn't fair of Desmond to ask. She was supposed to go back to Portland, register for school. Become a doctor like she'd dreamed about for over a decade. That's how she'd help people. This evisceration Desmond Pierce wanted to perform wasn't part of the plan.

"He might still need a kidney, too." Desmond shrugged. "Such is the nature of sharing DNA with another human."

Did he really not get the emotional quandary she was in? All of this must be so easy for him. After all, he was man, and rich besides—all he had to do was snap his fingers to make the world do his bidding. "You know breast-feeding isn't a one-time thing, right? You have to repeat it."

In the tight-knit community her parents belonged to, they raised babies as a village. She'd watched mothers commit to being a baby's sole food source twenty-four hours a day for months. Some women had trouble with breast-feeding. He acted like she could just pop out a breast and everything would be peachy.

"Yes, but once we find an alternative, you can walk away. Until then, our agreement means you have a commitment to his medical needs." He crossed his arms. "There is literally nothing I would not do to help my child. He needs you. Three months, at least. You can live with me, have your own room. Use a breast pump if you like. You want extra compensation added to the settlement? Name your price."

As if she could put a price on the maternal instincts that warred with her conviction that whatever decision she made here would have lasting impacts that neither of them could foresee. "I don't want extra compensation! I want—"

Nothing except what he'd already promised her. A divorce settlement that would pay for medical school and the knowledge that she'd helped him create the family he wanted. It felt so cold all at once. But what was she supposed to do instead? She rarely dated, not after three years with a ho-hum high school boyfriend and a pregnancy scare at nineteen, which was why she refused to go out with one of the men her parents were constantly throwing at her. Dating wasn't worth the possibility of an accidental pregnancy.

She couldn't be a mom and a doctor. Both required commitment, an exhaustive number of hours. So she'd chosen long ago which path worked for her. Because she was selfish, according to her mother, throwing away her parents' teaching about natural remedies as if their beliefs didn't matter.

So here was her chance to be unselfish for once. She could breast-feed for three months, wean the baby as he grew out of his formula allergy and go back to Portland for the spring semester. It was only a small addition to what had already been a year-long delay.

She'd wanted to experience pregnancy to better empathize with her patients. Why not experience breast-feeding for the same reason? She could use a pump if the baby had trouble latching on, just like any new mother. No one had to know that it was going to kill her to give up the baby a second time after she'd fallen the rest of the way in love with him.

She glanced up at Desmond, who was watching her hold the baby with an expression she couldn't interpret. "I'll do it. But you can't stay in the room."

His expression didn't change. "I beg to differ. He's my son."

Great, so now he was going to watch. But she could still dictate her own terms. "Can you at least call the nurse back so I can make sure I'm doing it right?"

Instead of forcing her to push the call button, he nodded and disappeared into the hall, giving her a blessed few moments alone. The hospital gown had slits for exactly this purpose so it was easy to maneuver the baby's face to her aching breast. His cries had quieted to heartbreaking mewls, and his eyes were closed, but his mouth worked the closer she guided him toward her nipple. And then all at once, he popped on like a champ and started sucking.

She was doing it. *He* was doing it.

Entranced, she watched her son take his first meal on this planet and it was almost holy. Her body flooded with a sense of rightness and awe. An eternity passed and a small sound caused her to glance up. Desmond had returned with the nurse, but he was just watching her quietly with far more tenderness than she would have expected.

"Looks like you're a natural, hon," the nurse said encouragingly and smiled. "In a few minutes, you can switch sides. Do you want me to stay?"

"I think I'm okay."

Really, fetching the nurse had been an excuse to get Desmond out of the room. Women had been doing this for centuries, including those of her parents' community who were strong advocates for removing the stigma of public breast-feeding. She wasn't a frail fraidy-cat.

The nurse left. Now that the baby was quiet, she felt Desmond's presence a whole lot more than she had before, like an extra weight had settled around her shoulders. He was so…everything. Intense. Focused. Gorgeous. Unsettling. Every time she glanced at him, it did something funny to her stomach and she'd had enough new sensations for the day, thanks.

Instead she watched the baby eat in silence until she couldn't stand it any longer.

"What did you name him?" Her voice was husky and drew Desmond's attention.

He cocked his head, his gaze traveling over her in a way that made her twitchy. "Conner. His middle name is Clark, after your father."

That speared her right through the heart. She'd had no idea he'd do something to honor his son's maternal heritage, and it struck her as personal in a way that dug under her skin. If all had gone according to plan, she'd never have met Desmond, never have known what he'd called the baby. She wouldn't have looked them up or contacted either of them. Also according to their agreement.

Now it was all backward and upside-down because this was their son. And Desmond Pierce was her husband. She'd just agreed to go home with him. How was that going to work? Would he expect to exercise his husbandly duties?

That thought flittered through her stomach in a way that wasn't difficult to interpret at all. Dear God. She was *attracted* to her husband. And she'd take that secret to the grave.

Mortified, she switched breasts under Desmond's watchful eye, figuring that if she would be living with him, he'd see her feeding the baby plenty of times. Besides, there was nothing shameful about a woman's body in the act of providing nourishment for her son. Somehow, though, Desmond made the whole thing seem intimate and heavy with implication, as if they were a real family and he was there to support his child's mother.

Desmond pursed his lips, still surveying her as if trying to figure something out. "Have we met before?"

Her pulse leaped. "No. Of course not. You wanted everything done through your agent."

Mr. Lively had been anything but. He was about a hundred and twenty years old and spoke slower than a tortoise on Valium. Anytime he'd contacted her about paperwork or medical records, she'd mentally blocked off four hours because that's generally how long the session lasted. Except for when she'd gone with him to the courthouse to complete the marriage by proxy, which had taken all day.

Suddenly she wished they'd done this surrogacy arrangement a different way. But marriage had been the easiest way to avoid legal issues. The divorce settlement, which she'd use to pay for school, was a normal agreement between couples with Desmond's kind of wealth. Otherwise someone could argue Desmond had paid for a baby and no one wanted that legal hassle.

She hadn't minded being technically married when it

was just a piece of paper. Meeting Desmond, being near enough to hear him breathe, changed everything. It felt bigger than a signature on an official document.

"You seem familiar." He shook his head as if clearing it. "It's been a long day."

"You don't say," she said, letting the irony drip from her tone. "I've been here since 3:00 a.m."

"Really?" This seemed to intrigue him.

"Yeah, it's not a drive-through. I was in labor for something like fifteen hours."

"Is that normal?"

She sighed and tried to shift her position without disturbing the baby. "I don't know. This is my first rodeo."

"I'm being insensitive."

Nothing like calling a spade a spade, which McKenna appreciated enough to give him a break. "I'm sure we'll get to know each other soon enough."

Somehow she'd managed to startle him. "Will we?"

"Well, sure, if we're living in the same house."

And she could secretly admit to a curiosity about him that she'd have every right to satisfy if they were in close quarters. There was a certain amount of protection in the fact that her time with him had predefined boundaries. The last thing she needed was additional entanglements that kept her from fulfilling her dreams. "But only for three months, right?"

"We'll do our best to keep it to three months," he said with a sharp nod, but she had the distinct impression he hadn't considered that inviting her to live in his house meant they'd be around each other. What exactly had she signed up for?

It didn't matter. All that mattered was that he'd given her three months with her son that she was pathetically grateful for. It was like a gift, a chance to know him before he grew old enough to remember her, to miss her. A chance to revel in all these newfound maternal instincts and then leave before they grew too strong. She was going to be a doctor, thanks to Desmond Pierce, and she couldn't let his monkey wrench change that.

Two

The house Desmond had lived in for the last ten years was not big enough. Twenty thousand square feet shouldn't feel so closed in. But with McKenna Moore inside his walls, everything shrank.

He'd never brought a woman home to live. Sure, Lacey had stayed over occasionally when they were dating, but her exit was always prearranged. And then she'd forever snuffed out his ability to trust a woman as easily as she'd snuffed out the life of their "accident," as she'd termed it. The baby had been unplanned, definitely, since their relationship hadn't been all that serious, but he'd had no idea how much he'd want the baby until it was too late. He'd always made sure there was a light at the end of the tunnel when it came to his interaction with women after that.

There was no light where his baby's mother was concerned. She'd brought her feminine scent and shiny dark hair into his house and put a stamp of permanence all over everything.

Did she know that he'd made a huge concession when he'd asked her to stay with him? This was his domain, his sanctuary, and he'd let her invade it, sucking up all the space while she was at it. Only for Conner would he have done this.

This, of course, looked an awful lot like he was hiding in his workshop. But he couldn't be in the main part of the house and walk around with the semi-erection McKenna gave him by simply laughing. Or looking at him. Or breathing. It was absurd. He'd been around women before. Gorgeous women who liked his money enough to put up with his idiosyncrasies. None of them had ever invoked such a driving need.

He tried to pretend he was simply working. After all, he often holed up in his workshop for days until Mrs. Elliot reminded him that he couldn't live on the Red Bull and Snickers that he kept in the corner refrigerator.

But there was a difference between hiding and holing up and he wasn't confused about which one he was doing. Apparently he was the only one who was clear on it, though, because the next time he glanced up from the robot hand he was rewiring, there *she* stood.

"Busy?" she called in her husky voice that hit with a solid *thwang* he felt in his gut.

"Ms. Moore," he muttered in acknowledgment. "This is my workshop."

"I know." Her brows quirked as she glanced around with unveiled curiosity. "Mrs. Elliot told me this was where I could find you. Also, we share a child. I think it's okay if you call me McKenna."

But she clearly didn't know "workshop" equaled off-limits, private, no girls allowed. He should post a sign.

"McKenna, then." He shouldn't be talking to her. Encouraging her. But he couldn't stop looking at her. She was gorgeous in a fierce, elemental way that coursed through him every time he got anywhere near her.

And when he stumbled over her breast-feeding? God, that was the worst. Or the best, depending on your viewpoint.

She was at her sexiest when she was nurturing their child. If he'd known he'd suddenly be ten times more drawn to her when she exuded all that maternal radiance, he'd never have invited her to live here.

Of course, he hadn't really had much of a choice there, had he?

Obviously hiding out wasn't the answer. Like always, raw need welled up as he watched her explore his workshop, peering into bins and tracing the lines of the hand-drawn gears posted to a light board near the south wall.

"This is a very impressive setup," she commented as she finished a round of his cavernous workspace.

Her gaze zipped to the two generators housed at the back and then lit on him as he stood behind the enormous workstation spread out over a mobile desk on wheels where he did all of his computation. He'd built the computer himself from components and there wasn't another like it in the world.

"It's where I make stuff," he told her simply because there was no way to explain that this was where he brought to life the contents of his brain. He saw something in his head then he built it. He'd been doing that since he was four. Now he got paid millions and millions of dollars for each and every design, which he only cared about because it enabled him to keep doing it.

"I can see that. It's kind of sexy. Very Dr. Frankenstein."

Had she just called him sexy? In the same breath as comparing him to *Frankenstein*? "Uh…I've always thought of myself as more like Iron Man."

She laughed. "Except Tony Stark is a lot more personable and dresses better."

Desmond glanced down at his slacks. "What's wrong with the way I dress?"

Certainly that was the only part of her assessment he could disagree with—he was by no stretch personable and Iron Man did have a certain flair that Desmond could never claim.

"Nothing," she shot back with a grin. "You just don't look like a billionaire playboy who does weapons deals with shady Middle Eastern figures. Frankenstein, on the other hand, was a doctor like you and all he wanted to do was build something meaningful out of the pieces he had available."

She picked up the robot hand he'd been about to solder for emphasis.

Speechless, he stared at her slender fingers wrapped around his creation-in-progress and tried like hell to figure out how she'd tapped into his psyche so easily. Fascinating. So few people thought of him as a doctor. He didn't even see himself as one, despite the fact that he could stick *PhD* after his name all day long if he wanted to.

What else did she see when she looked at him? That same recognition he'd felt, as if they'd met in a former life and their connection had been so strong it transcended flesh and bone?

Or would that sound as crazy to her as it did in his head?

"I wasn't aware I was so transparent," he said gruffly, a little shocked that he didn't totally hate it. "Did you want something?"

Her dark eyes were so expressive he could practically read her like a book. He rarely bothered to study people anymore. Once, that had been the only way he could connect with others, by surreptitiously observing them until everything was properly cataloged.

All it had ever gotten him was an acute sense of isolation and an understanding that people stayed away from him because they didn't like how his brain worked.

She shrugged. "I was bored. Larissa is putting Conner to bed and it turns out that having a nanny around means that once I feed him, I'm pretty much done. I haven't seen you in, like, a week."

McKenna, apparently, had no such aversion to Desmond. She'd sought him out. So he could entertain her. That was a first.

"I had no idea you'd mark my absence in such a way."

Lame. He was out of practice talking to people, let alone one who tied his brain in a Gordian knot of puzzling reactions.

But he wanted to untangle that knot. Very badly.

"Are you always so formal?" McKenna came around the long table to his side and peered over his shoulder at the monitor where he had a drawing of the robot hand spinning in 3-D. "Wow. That's pretty cool."

"It's just a… No, I'm not—" He sucked in a breath as her torso grazed his back. His pulse roared into overdrive and he experienced a purely primal reaction to her that had no place between two people who shared a son and nothing else. "Formal."

"Hmm? Oh, yeah, you are. You remind me of my statistics professor."

"You took a statistics class?" Okay, they shared that, too. But that was it. They had nothing else in common and he had no reason to be imagining her reaction if he kissed her.

"Have to. It's a requirement for premed."

"Can you not stand there?"

Her scent was bleeding through his senses and it was thoroughly disrupting his brain waves. Of course the real problem was that he liked her exactly where she was.

"Where? Behind you?" She punched him on the shoulder like they were drinking buddies and she'd just told him a joke. "I can't be in front of you. There's a whole lot of electronic equipment in my way."

"You talk a lot."

She laughed. "Only because you're talking back. Isn't that how it works?"

For the second time she'd rendered him speechless. Yeah. He *was* talking back. The two conversations he'd had with her to date, the one at the hospital and this one, marked the longest he'd had with anyone in a while. Probably since Lacey.

He needed someone to draw him out, or he stayed stuck in his head, designing, building, imagining, dreaming. It was a lot safer for everyone that way, so of course that was his default.

McKenna seemed unacquainted with the term *boundaries*. And he didn't hate that.

He should. He should be escorting her out of his workshop and back to the main part of the house. There was an indoor pool that stayed precisely the same temperature year-round. A recreational room that he'd had built the moment Mr. Lively called to say McKenna had conceived during the first round of insemination. Desmond had filled the room with a pool table, darts, video game consoles and whatever else the decorator had recommended. Surely his child's mother could find some amusement there.

"Tell me what you're building," she commanded with a fair enough amount of curiosity that he told her.

"It's a prototype for a robotic humanoid."

"A robot?" Clearly intrigued, she leaned over the hand, oblivious to the way her hair fell in a long, dark sheet over her shoulder. It was so beautiful that he almost reached out to touch it.

He didn't. That would invite intimacies he absolutely wanted with a bone-deep desire but hadn't fully yet analyzed. Until he understood this visceral need, he couldn't act on it. Too dangerous. It gave her too much power.

"No." He cleared his throat and scrubbed at his beard, which he still hadn't trimmed. "A robot is anything mechanical that can be programmed. A robotic humanoid resembles a person both in appearance and function but with a mechanical skeleton and artificial intelligence."

It was a common misconception that he corrected often, especially when he had to give a presentation about his designs to the manufacturers who bought his patents.

"You *are* Dr. Frankenstein," she said with raised eyebrows. "When you get it to work, do you shout 'It's alive!' or just do a little victory dance?"

"I, um…"

She'd turned to face him, crossing her arms under her breasts that he logically knew were engorged from childbirth, though that didn't seem to stop his imagination from calling up what they looked like: expanses of beautiful flesh topped by hard, dusky nipples. McKenna had miles of skin that Des wanted to put his hands on.

What was it about her that called to him so deeply?

"I'm just teasing you." Her eyes twinkled. "I actually couldn't imagine you doing either one."

A smile spread across his face before he could stop it. "I can dance."

"Ha, you're totally lying."

"I can dance," he repeated. "Just not to music."

He fell into her rich, dark eyes and he reached out to snag a lock of her hair, fingering the silky softness before he fully realized that he'd given in to the impulse. The moment grew tense. Aware. So thick, he couldn't have cut it with a laser.

"I should...go," she murmured and blinked, unwinding the spell. "I didn't mean to interrupt."

The lock of hair fell from his fingers as the mood shattered. Fortunately her exodus was quick enough that she didn't get to witness how well she'd bobbled his composure.

He'd have sworn there was an answering echo of attraction and heat in her gaze.

He wasn't any closer to unraveling the mysteries lurking inside her, but he did know one thing. McKenna Moore had taken his seed into her womb and created a miracle through artificial insemination.

What had once felt practical now felt like a mistake. One he couldn't rectify.

But how could he have known he'd take one look at her and wish he'd impregnated her by making love over and over and over until she'd conceived?

Madness. *Build something and forget all of this fatalistic nonsense.*

Women were treacherous under the best of circumstances and McKenna Moore was no different. She just had a unique wrapper that rendered Des stupid, apparently.

Of course the most expedient way to nip this attraction in the bud would be to tell her how badly he'd wanted to thread all of his fingers through her hair and kiss her until her clothes melted off. She'd be mortified and finally figure out that she should be running away from Desmond Pierce. That would be that.

McKenna fled Desmond's workshop, her pulse still pounding in her throat.

What the hell had just happened? One minute she was trying to forge a friendship with the world's most reclusive billionaire and the next he had her hair draped across his hand.

She could still feel the tug as his fingers lifted the strands. The look on his face had been enthralled, as if he'd unexpectedly found gold. She hadn't been around the block very many times, a testament to how long she'd been with James, her high school boyfriend, not to mention the years of difficult undergraduate course work that hadn't allowed for much time to date. But she knew when a man was thinking about kissing her, and that's exactly what had been on Desmond's mind.

That would be a huge mistake.

She needed to walk out of this house in three months unencumbered, emotionally and physically, and Desmond was dangerous. He held all the cards in this scenario and if she wanted to dedicate her life to medicine, she had to be careful. What would happen if she accidentally got pregnant again? More delays. More agonizing decisions and, frankly, she didn't have enough willpower left to deal with those kinds of consequences.

And what made her near mistake even worse was that she'd almost forgotten why she was there. She'd fallen into borderline flirting that was nothing like how she usually was with men. But Desmond was darkly mysterious and intriguing in a way she found sexy, totally against her will. They shared an almost mystical connection, one she'd never felt before, and it was as scary as it was fascinating.

Okay. Seeking him out had been an error in judgment. Obviously. But they never crossed paths and she was starting to wonder if she'd imagined that she'd come home from the hospital with a man. It only made sense that she should be on friendly terms with her baby's father.

Why that made sense, she couldn't remember all at once. Desmond didn't want a mother for his son. Just a chuck wagon. Once she helped Conner wean, she'd finally be on track to get her medical degree after six arduous years as an undergrad and one grueling year spent prepping her body to get pregnant, being pregnant and then giving birth.

In a house this size, there was literally no reason she ever had to see Desmond again. She'd managed to settle in and live here for over a week without so much as a glimpse until she'd sought him out in his workshop.

Her days fell into a rhythm that didn't suck. Mrs. Elliot fed her and provided companionable but neutral conversation when McKenna prompted her. Clothes magically appeared cleaned and pressed in McKenna's closet. Twice a week, her beautifully decorated bedroom and the adjoining bathroom were unobtrusively cleaned. All in all, she was drowning in luxury. And she wouldn't apologize for enjoying it.

To shed the baby weight that had settled around her hips and stomach, she'd started swimming in the pool a couple of hours a day. Before she'd gotten pregnant, she'd jogged. But there were no trails through the heavy forest of hemlocks and maples that surrounded this gothic mansion perched at the edge of the Columbia River. Even if she found a place to run, her enormous breasts hurt when she did something overly taxing, like breathing and thinking. She could only imagine how painful it would be to jog three miles.

The pool was amazing, huge and landscaped with all sorts of indoor plants that made her feel like she was at a tropical oasis on another continent instead of in north-west Oregon where she'd spent the whole of her life. A glass ceiling let in light but there were no windows to break the illusion. She could swim uninterrupted for as long as she liked. It was heavenly.

Until she emerged from the water one day and wiped her face to see Desmond sitting on one of the lounge chairs, quietly watching her. She hadn't seen him since the workshop incident a week ago that might have been an almost kiss.

"Hey," she called, mystified why her pulse leaped into overdrive the second her senses registered his presence. "Been here long?"

"Long enough," he said cryptically, his smooth voice echoing in the cavernous pool area. "Am I disturbing you?"

He'd sought her out, clearly, since he wasn't dressed for swimming and wore an expectant expression.

So she lied. "Of course not."

In reality he did disturb her. A lot. His eyes matched his name, piercing her to the bone when he looked at her, and she didn't like how shivery and goose-pimply he turned her mostly bare skin. There was something about him she couldn't put her finger on, but the man had more shadows than a graveyard. She could see them flitting around in his expression, in his demeanor, as if they weighed him down.

Until he smiled. And thank God he didn't do that more

often, because he went from sexy in an abstract way to holy-crap hot.

So she'd do everything in her power to not make him smile for however long he planned to grace her with his presence. Hopefully that would only be a few minutes. If she'd known he was going to make an appearance, she'd have brought something to cover her wet swimsuit, like a full suit of armor made of inch-thick chain mail.

The way he was looking at her made her feel exposed.

She settled for a towel, draping it around her torso like a makeshift toga, which at least covered her pointy nipples, and sat on the next lounge chair, facing him.

Desmond was wearing a white button-down shirt today, with the sleeves rolled to his forearms and, despite teasing him the other day about his fashion sense, he had such a strange, magnetic aura that she scarcely noticed anything extraneous like clothes. All she saw was him.

"Are you settling in okay?" he asked.

She had the sense the question wasn't small talk. "Sure. What's not to like?"

His eyebrows quirked. "The fact that you're here in the first place."

"You're making it worth my while, remember?"

That shouldn't have come out so sarcastically. After all, she'd been the one to shake her head at monetary compensation, which he'd likely have readily ponied up.

But he was making her twitchy with his shadowy gaze. After visiting his workshop, she'd looked up the things he'd invented and his mind was definitely not like other people's. Innovation after innovation in the areas of robotics and machinery had spilled onto her screen along with published papers full of his endless theoretical ideas.

She was not a stupid person by any stretch, having graduated with a bachelor's degree in biology and a 3.5

grade point average, but Desmond Pierce existed on another plane. And that made him thoroughly out of reach to mere mortals like her.

But he was still oh, so intriguing. And they were married. Funny how that had become front and center in her mind all at once.

He nodded. "I'm sorry my request has delayed your own plans."

Clearly he didn't get offended by her jokes that weren't funny. That was a good thing.

"I have my whole life to be a doctor. Conner will only be a newborn for this small stretch of time."

It was a huge concession, and she had her own reasons for being there, none of which she planned to share with Conner's father. But her pathetic gratefulness for this time with her son wouldn't go away, no matter how hard she tried to think of breast-feeding as a task instead of the bonding experience it was proving to be.

Conner would not be her son legally once Desmond filed the divorce decree that spelled out the custody arrangement—she'd give up all rights. Period. End of story. She hated how often she had to remind herself of that. She was already dreading the inevitable goodbye that would be here long before she wished.

"That's true. I do appreciate your willingness, regardless."

"Is that the only reason you popped in here? To thank me?" She flashed a grin before thinking better of it. They weren't friends hanging out, even though it seemed too easy to forget that. "I would have taken a text message."

"I despise text messages."

"Really?" Curiously, she eyed him. "Electronic communication seems like it would be right up your alley."

He shifted uncomfortably, breaking eye contact. "Why, because I'm not as verbally equipped as others?"

"Please." She snorted before realizing he was serious. "There's nothing about you that's ill equipped. I meant because you're the Frankenstein of electronics."

Thoughtfully, he absorbed that comment and she could see it pinging around in his brain, looking for a place to land. Then he shrugged. "I don't like text messages because they're intrusive and distracting, forcing me to respond."

"You can ignore them if you want," she advised and bit back another smile. Sometimes he was so cute. "There's no rule."

"There is. It's like a social contract I have to fulfill. The message sits there and blinks and blinks until I read it. And then I know exactly who is sitting on the other end waiting on me to complete the transaction. I can't just let that go." His brows came together. "That's why I don't give people my cell phone number."

"I have your cell phone number."

"You're not people."

She couldn't help it. She laughed. And that apparently gave him permission to smile, which was so gorgeous she had a purely physical reaction to it. Somehow he must have picked up on the sharp tug through her insides because the vibe between them got very heavy, very fast.

Mesmerized, she stared at him as the smiles slipped off both their faces.

Why was she so attracted to him? He wasn't her type. Actually she didn't have a type because she'd spent the last six years working her ass off to earn a four-year degree, putting herself through college with as many flexible retail and restaurant jobs as she could score. She couldn't do the same for medical school, not unless she wanted to be fifty when she graduated.

She had to remember that this man held the keys to her future and to keep her wits about her.

Desmond cleared his throat and the moment faded. "I didn't seek you out to talk about text messages. I wanted to let you know that Larissa has resigned her position. Effective immediately."

"The nanny quit?" That sucked. She'd liked Larissa and had thoroughly approved of Desmond's choice. "And with no notice? Nice. Did she at least give you a reason?"

"Her mother had a stroke. She felt compelled to be the one managing her mother's care."

"Well, okay. That gets a pass."

Unexpectedly, McKenna's eyelids pricked in sympathy as she imagined her own mother in a similar circumstance, lifeless and hooked up to machines as the doctors performed analysis to determine the extent of the brain damage the stroke had caused. Of course, her mother would have refused to be cared for in a real hospital, stubborn to the end, even if it led to her own grave. Like it had for Grandfather, who had shared the beliefs of their community.

McKenna was the outcast who put her faith in science and technology.

"She did the right thing," McKenna said. "Have you started the process of hiring a replacement?"

"I have. I contacted the service I used to find Larissa and they're sending me the résumés of some candidates. I'd hoped you'd review them with me."

"Me?" Oh, God. He wanted her to help him pick the woman who would essentially raise her child? How could she do that?

A thousand emotions flew through her at once as Desmond nodded.

"It would be helpful if you would, yes," he said, oblivious to her shock and disquiet.

"You did fine the first time without me," she squawked and cleared her throat. "You don't need my help."

"The first time I had nine months to select the right person for the job," he countered. "I have one day this time. And I trust your judgment."

"You do?" That set her back so much that she sagged against the weave of the lounge chair.

"Of course. You're intelligent, or you wouldn't have been accepted into medical school, and you have a unique ability to understand people."

She frowned. "I do not. Mostly I piss people off."

Her mouth was far too fast to express exactly what was on her mind, and she did not suffer fools easily. Neither made her very popular with men, which was fine by her. Men were just roadblocks she did not have time for.

Desmond cocked his head in the way she'd come to realize meant he was processing what she'd just said. "You don't make me mad."

"That's because I like you," she muttered before thinking through how that might come across. Case in point. Her mouth often operated independently of her brain.

His expression closed in, dropping shadows between them again. "That will change soon enough. I'm not easy to get along with, nor should you try. There's a reason I asked you to be my son's surrogate."

She should let it go. The shadows weren't her business and he'd pretty much just told her to back off. But the mystery of Desmond Pierce had caught her by the throat and she couldn't stop herself from asking since he'd brought up the subject.

"Why *did* you ask me?"

Surely a rich, good-looking guy could have women crawling out of the woodwork to be his baby mama with the snap of his fingers. Obviously that wasn't what he'd wanted.

Coolly, he surveyed her. "Because I dislike not having control. Our agreement means you have no rights and no ability to affect what happens to Conner."

"But I do," she countered quietly. "You put me in exactly that position by asking me to breast-feed him. I could walk away tomorrow and it would be devastating for you both."

"Yes. It is an unfortunate paradox. But it should give you an idea how greatly I care about my son that I am willing to make such a concession. I didn't do it lightly."

Geez. His jaw was like granite and she had an inkling why he considered himself difficult to get along with. Desmond didn't want a mother for his son because he wasn't much of a sharer.

Good to know. Domineering geniuses weren't her cup of tea. "Well, we have no problems, then. I'm not interested in pulling the parental rug out from under you. I'm helping you out because I'm the only one who can, but I'm really looking forward to medical school."

This time with Conner and Desmond was just a detour. It had to be, no matter how deep her son might sink his emotional hooks.

Desmond nodded. "That is why I picked you. Mr. Lively did a thorough screening of all the potential surrogates and your drive to help people put you head and shoulders above the rest. Your principles are your most attractive quality."

Um…what? She blinked, but the sincerity in his expression didn't change. Had he just called her attractive because of her stubborn need to do things her own way? That was a first. And it warmed her dangerously fast.

Her parents had lambasted those same principles for as long as she could recall, begging her to date one of the men who lived in their community and have a lot of babies, never mind that she had less than no interest in either concept. The men bored her to tears, not to mention they embraced her parents' love of alternative medicine, which meant she had nothing in common with them.

How great was it that the man she'd ultimately married appreciated her desire to become a medical doctor instead of a homeopathic healer?

And how terrible to realize that Desmond Pierce had chosen her strictly because he expected she'd easily leave her child without a backward glance.

He was right—she would do it because she'd given her word. But there wasn't going to be anything easy about it.

Three

Since the nanny had left him high and dry, Desmond was the one stuck sorting out his son's 3:00 a.m. meltdown. Conner woke yowling for God knew what reason. Larissa had always taken care of that in the past, leaving Des blessedly ignorant to his son's needs.

Unfortunately, after twenty minutes of rocking, soothing, toys and terse commands, nothing had worked to stop the crying. If he'd known Conner would pull this kind of stunt, Des would have gone to bed before 1:00 a.m. Two hours of sleep did not make this easier, that was for sure.

Desmond finally conceded that he no longer had the luxury of pretending McKenna didn't exist just to keep his growing attraction to her under wraps. Larissa's printed instructions clearly said the baby nursed at night. He'd been hoping for a miracle that would prevent him from having to disturb Conner's mother. That did not happen.

So that's how he found himself knocking on her door in the dead of night with a crying baby in his arms. Definitely not the way he'd envisioned seeing McKenna Moore in a bedroom. And he'd had more than a few fantasies about McKenna and a bed.

She answered a minute later, dressed in a conservative white robe that shouldn't have been the slightest bit alluring. It absolutely was, flashing elegant bits of leg as she leaned into the puddle of light from the hall.

"Woke up hungry, did he?" she said with more humor than Des expected at three in the morning. "Give him here," she instructed and, when he handed over the baby, cradled him to her bosom, murmuring as she floated to an overstuffed recliner in the corner of her room.

Funny. He hadn't realized until this moment that she sat in it to feed Conner. He'd envisioned her snuggling deep into the crevices to read a book or to chat on the phone with her legs draped over the sides. McKenna seemed like the type to lounge in a chair instead of sitting in it properly.

The lamp on the small end table cast a circle of warmth over the chair as she settled into it and worked open her robe to feed the baby. Instantly, Conner latched on and grew quiet.

"You can come in if you want," McKenna called to Desmond as he stood like an idiot at the door, completely extraneous and completely unable to walk away.

"I would…like to come in," he clarified and cleared his throat because his voice sounded like a hundred frogs had crawled down his windpipe. Gingerly, he sat on the bed because the love seat that matched the recliner was too close to mother and child.

Similar to the other times he'd watched McKenna breast-feed, he couldn't quite get over the initial shock of the mechanics. It was one thing to have an academic understanding of lactation, but quite another to see it in action.

Especially when he had such a strong reaction, like he was witnessing something divine.

The beauty of it filled him and he couldn't look away, even as she repositioned the baby and her dark nipple flashed. God, that shouldn't be so affecting. This woman was feeding his son in the most sacrificial of ways. But neither could he deny the purely physical reaction he had to her naked breast.

He couldn't stop being unnaturally attracted to her any more than he could stop the sun from rising. Seeing her with Conner only heightened that attraction.

Mother and child together created a package he liked.

He shouldn't have stayed. But he couldn't have left.

This quandary he was in had to stop. McKenna would be out of his life in two months and he'd insist that she not contact him again. Hell, he probably wouldn't have to insist. She was resolute in her goal of becoming a doctor, as they'd discussed at the pool yesterday.

In the meantime he'd drive himself insane if he didn't get their relationship, such as it was, on better footing. There was absolutely no reason they couldn't have a working rapport as they took care of the baby together. At least until he hired a new nanny.

"Is it okay that I brought him to you?" he asked gruffly. "I don't know what you worked out with Larissa."

He felt like he should be doing more to care for his son. But all he could do was make sure the woman who could feed him was happy.

"Perfectly fine. She's been trying a bottle at night with different types of formula to see if she can get his stomach to accept it when he's good and hungry. Hasn't worked so far." McKenna shrugged one shoulder, far too chipper for having been woken unceremoniously in the middle of the night. "So I take over when she gets frustrated."

"She didn't mention that in her instructions." Probably distracted with trying to pack and deal with travel arrangements on such short notice. So he reeled back his annoyance that he hadn't followed the routine his son was probably used to. It wasn't anyone's fault.

Clearly he needed to take a more active role in caring for Conner. This was the perfect opportunity to get clued in on whatever Larissa and McKenna had been doing thus far.

"Taking care of a baby is kind of a moving target," she said.

"Speaking from your years of experience?" He hadn't meant for that to come out sarcastically.

But she just laughed, which he appreciated far more than he should.

"I come from a very tight-knit community. We raise our babies together. I've been taking care of other people's children for as long as I can remember."

Mr. Lively had briefed him thoroughly on the cooperative community tucked into the outskirts of the Clatsop Forest where McKenna had grown up. Her unusual upbringing had been one of the reasons she'd stood out among the women he'd considered for his surrogate. "Surprising, then, that you'd be willing to give one up."

She contemplated him for a moment. "But that's why I was willing. I've seen firsthand what having a child does to a mother's time and energy. You become its everything and there's little left over for anything else, like your husband, let alone medical school, a grueling residency and then setting up a practice."

"It's not like that for you here, is it?"

"No, of course not." She flashed him a smile. "For one, we're not involved."

He couldn't resist pulling that thread. "What if we were?"

The concept hung there, writhing between them like a live thing, begging to be explored. And he wasn't going to take it back. He wanted to know more about her, what made her tick.

"What? Involved?"

The idea intrigued her. He could read it in her expressive eyes. But then she banked it.

"That's the whole point, Desmond. We never would have had a child together under any other circumstances. You wanted to be a single father for your own reasons, but whatever they are, the reality is that neither of us has room in our lives for getting *involved*."

A timely reminder, one he shouldn't have needed.

Even so, he couldn't help thinking he was going about this process wrong. Instead of hiding out in his lab until he'd fully analyzed his attraction to McKenna, he should create an environment to explore it. That was the only way he could understand it well enough to make it stop. What better conditions could he ask for than plenty of time together and an impending divorce?

"As long as you're happy while you're here," he said as his mind instantly turned that over. "That's all that matters to me."

He was nothing if not imaginative, and when he wanted something, there was little that could stop him from devising a way to get it. One of the many benefits of being a genius.

She glanced up at him after repositioning the baby. "You know what would make me happy? Finding a nanny with an expertise in weaning when the baby has formula allergies."

"Then, tomorrow, that's what we'll do," he promised her.

And if that endeavor included getting to know his child's mother in a much more intimate way, then *everyone* would be happy.

The next morning, McKenna woke to a beep that signaled an incoming text message.

She sat up and reached for her phone, instantly awake despite having rolled around restlessly for an hour after Desmond had left her room with the baby.

Definitely not the way she'd envisioned him visiting her bedroom in the middle of the night, though she shouldn't be having such vivid fantasies about her husband. Hard not to when she'd developed a weird habit of dreaming about him—especially when she was awake—and fantasies weren't so easy to shut off when she had little to occupy her time other than feeding the baby.

Desmond's name leaped out at her from the screen. He'd sent her a text message.

That shouldn't make her smile. But she couldn't help picturing him phone in hand as he fat-fingered his way through what should be simple communication.

Come to my workshop when you're free.

God, he was so adorable. Why that made her mushy inside, she had no clue. But, obviously, he didn't realize she was bored out of her mind pretty much all the time.

She was definitely free. Especially if it meant she got to visit Frankenstein's wonderland again.

She brushed her hair and washed her face. Rarely did she bother with cosmetics as she'd been blessed with really great skin that needed little to stay supple and blemish free. Why mess with it?

In less than five minutes, she was ready to go downstairs. Desmond glanced up from his computer nearly the moment she walked through the glass door of his workshop. "That was fast."

She shrugged casually, or as casually as she could when faced with a man she'd last seen in the middle of the night while she'd been half-naked. "I'm at your beck and call, right?"

Something flashed through his expression that added a few degrees to the temperature. "Are you? I thought you were here for Conner."

"That's what I meant," she corrected hastily, lest he get the wrong idea.

Though judging by the way he was looking at her, it was already too late. He was such a strange mix of personality, sometimes warm and inviting, other times prickly. But always fascinating. And she liked pushing his buttons.

She *shouldn't* be pushing any buttons.

Desmond was not her type. There were far too many complications at play here to indulge in the rising heat between them. "But apparently I can be persuaded to make myself available to his father, as well. Pending the subject of discussion, of course."

Desmond crossed his arms and leaned back in his chair, his expression decidedly warmer. "What would you like to talk about?"

She shrugged and bit back the flirtatious comment

on the tip of her tongue. She was pretty sure he hadn't summoned her to pick up where they'd left off the last time she'd made the mistake of cornering him in his workshop—when she'd been convinced he was about to kiss her.

"I figured you had something specific you wanted. Since you crawled out of the Dark Ages to send me a text."

The corners of his mouth lifted in a small smile that shouldn't have tingled her spine the way it did.

"Isn't that your preferred method of communication? I can adapt."

The ambience in the workshop was definitely different than the normal vibe between them. If she didn't know better, she'd think he was flirting with her. "You don't strike me as overly flexible. Maybe I should be adapting to you."

His gaze narrowed, sharpening, making her feel very much like a small, tasty rabbit. Never one to let a man make her feel hunted, she breached the space between them, skirting the long end of the worktable to put herself on the same side as Desmond.

Apparently she was going to let him push *her* buttons instead.

Last time she'd cornered him, he'd been guarded. Not this time. His crossed arms unknotted and fell to his sides, opening him to her perusal, and that was so interesting, she looked her fill. The man was beautifully built, with a long, lean torso and a classically handsome face made all the more dashing by a sparse beard. It was a perfect complement to his high cheekbones, allowing his gorgeous eyes to be the focal point.

"What would that look like?" he murmured. "If you adapted to me?"

"Oh, um…I don't know. How do you like to communicate?"

He jerked his head toward the back of the workshop
without taking his eyes off of her. "I build things. Shape
them, put the pieces where they go based on the images
I have in my head. I communicate through my hands."

Oh, God. That was the sexiest thing she'd ever heard
and her body didn't hesitate to flood her with the evidence of it, heating every millimeter of her skin as she
imagined the things he'd say to her via his fingertips.

"That sounds very effective." They weren't talking
about communication anymore and they both knew it.

He was definitely flirting with her. The question was
whether or not she wanted him to stop. This heat roil-
ing between them surely wasn't a good thing to encourage but, for the life of her, she couldn't remember why.

Oh, who was she kidding? The man intrigued the hell
out of her and she should just stop pretending otherwise.

"Sometimes," he said, his voice lowering a touch,
"more often than not, I'm misinterpreted."

"Maybe because whoever you're communicating with
isn't listening hard enough."

She'd definitely listen, if for no other reason than
to unlock some of his secrets. His mind fascinated her
and… Coupled with the body? He could definitely talk to
her all night long—with his hands, his mouth, whatever
he wanted to use—and she'd be okay with that.

No. That was a bad idea. This mystical draw between
them would not end well. She had goals. He was a con-
trolling, difficult-to-get-along-with recluse. They had
nothing between them but a son.

"Perhaps. But, generally speaking, people find me
hard to understand."

"I'm not people," she murmured instead of *see you*

later. "Why don't you tell me something and I'll let you know if I'm having trouble translating."

Delicious anticipation unfolded in her abdomen, the likes of which she hadn't felt in a long time. They shouldn't get involved. There were probably a hundred reasons their agreement would be altered if they did. Loopholes she'd never considered would bind her to this house simply because she lacked the will to step back from her husband.

He was so hypnotic she couldn't tear herself away from what was happening. She wanted to be right here in this moment, as long as it lasted.

Slowly he reached out and slid his fingers through her hair, examining it. Giving her time to hear what he was saying without uttering a word. He caught her in the crosshairs of his gaze as he fingered the lock and his expression told her he liked the dark, heavy mass that fell down her back.

She watched as he looped a wider hank around his palm, winding it up until his hand was near her face.

Desmond feathered a thumb across her cheek that drove a spike of need through her that was answered in the heat radiating from his eyes.

His other hand slid to her waist, slowly drawing her closer until their bodies brushed.

Oh, yes, she liked what he was saying.

Then he released her hair in favor of cupping her jaw with both hands and guiding her lips to his. The kiss instantly caught fire and she moaned as he tilted her head to take it deeper, levering open her lips with his. His tongue worked its way into her mouth, tasting her with intent, and she liked that, too, meeting him with her own taste test.

She wanted to touch. Resting her fingertips on his

chest, she indulged herself in the sensations of the crisp cotton and strong male torso underneath. His wild heartbeat thumped under her fingers as his lips shaped hers into new heights of pleasure.

God, yes, he was a hot kisser, communicating with his hands as promised. The heat of his palms on her flesh radiated through her whole body. The worktable bit into her back as he levered her against it, his granite-hard erection digging into her pelvis deliciously.

The unnatural attraction she'd felt for him from the start exploded. If she didn't stop this madness, they'd be naked in half a heartbeat. Not a smart move for a woman who wanted to walk out the door unencumbered in a few weeks.

That thought was enough to spur her brain into functioning.

She pulled back, but not very far since he still had her trapped between his body and the table. Her pulse thundered in her ears as they stared at each other.

"That was…"

"Amazing?" he supplied, his gaze still hot and clearly interested in diving in again. But he didn't, which she appreciated. "Yeah. But I'm sensing we're going to stop now."

"See, we communicate just fine." She gulped. "I'm just…not sure this is a good idea."

They were not two people who had the luxury of an uncomplicated fling. He'd expressed in no uncertain terms exactly how much control he liked having over a situation. They were married with a divorce agreement already hammered out. That was not a recipe for experimentation, and she wasn't much of an experimenter anyway.

Where could this possibly go?

"Oh, it's a good idea." His piercing gaze tore her open inside as he promised her exactly how good it would be without saying a word. "But we both have to think so."

With that, he stepped back, releasing her.

She took the first deep breath she'd taken since he'd told her he communicated with his hands and nodded. "I agree. And I don't think that right now."

Four

The kiss experiment hadn't worked out like Des had hoped in any way, shape or form. Instead of providing data on how he could stop the unholy allure of his wife, kissing her had opened an exponential number of dimensions to his attraction.

Worse, he wanted to do it again for purely unscientific reasons.

The feel of her mouth against his haunted him. He recalled it at the most inopportune times, like when he should be focusing on the metal pieces in front of him as he attempted to solder them to the titanium skeleton he was creating. So far, he'd had to start over three times. If he kept this up, the end result would look more like a grotesque spider hybrid than a human.

The problem his mind wanted to resolve didn't involve robotic humanoids. It involved how to kiss McKenna again. She'd backed off and then backed away. As he'd fully expected. Women in his world fell into two camps:

those who didn't think he was worth the trouble and those who did solely due to their own agenda.

His wife clearly fell into the first group.

Either way, *all* women considered him difficult. And McKenna was no exception. This was just the first time in memory that he cared. How could he get her to the point where she thought kissing was a good idea if she avoided him? As she surely had been; he hadn't seen her in two days.

He turned the dilemma over in his mind, getting nowhere with it. And nowhere with his prototype, which should be at least half finished by now. Salvation came via an email from the nanny-placement service.

Excellent. The list of candidates scrolled onto the screen. There was nothing he liked better than data unless it was even more data. The only way to make a reasonable decision was to weigh variables and risks, then chart all of that into potential outcomes. What a great distraction from his unfinished work.

Better than that, the nanny candidates were an *excuse*. He'd asked McKenna for her help in weeding out the potentials for a number of reasons, not the least of which was that she had a vested interest in ensuring the nanny had lactation and weaning experience. And he did appreciate the way McKenna's mind worked. Handy that he'd have to spend time with her to discuss the résumés. Maybe at the same time, he could get closer to that next kiss. The pluses of this task were legion.

Except when he sought her out, he found her in the solarium feeding the baby. God, why did the sight of her with Conner at her breast whack him so hard every time? He should be used to it after the handful of occasions he'd been present for the event.

Nope.

"Sorry," he offered gruffly when she glanced up and caught him skulking at the entrance to the solarium at the west end of the house, positioned just so to catch the late-afternoon sun. "I can come back."

"This is your house. *You're* free to come and go at will," she reminded him as if he needed the reminder that she was here under duress.

"You should feel as if you can move about at will, as well." At a loss as to why this whole scene was making him uncomfortable, he ran a palm over his beard, but it didn't jog his rusty people skills. "Do you need something from me to solidify that for you?"

"No." She sighed and focused on Conner for a long moment. "I'm sorry, I'm being weird."

Biting back a laugh because that shouldn't be so funny, he shook his head. "That's usually my line. You are far from weird."

She made a face. "You're not weird either. And I meant since, you know…the other day happened, we're in a strange place."

The other day. When he'd kissed her. As he worked through several responses to that in his head, he contemplated her. She flushed and fiddled with the baby's placement, shifting him around until he was precisely in the same spot he had been before she'd started.

Interesting. She was as uncomfortable as he was. Why?

Fascinated, he crossed his arms, instantly more interested in staying than in fleeing for the safety of his lab where everything worked the way he willed it to. "Not so strange of a place. We're still married, the baby still needs breast milk and I still need a nanny. What's weird about that?"

"You know what I mean," she muttered.

"Maybe I don't." Social norms escaped him on a regular basis. But he was starting to enjoy the rush of endorphins his body produced when around her. As long as he kept a tight rein on it.

"Then never mind," she said with a frown. "Obviously the weirdness is all on my side. I guess you just go around kissing people randomly whenever you feel like it and it never costs you a wink of sleep."

Well, now that *was* interesting information. "You're having trouble sleeping? Because I kissed you? Why?"

He definitely would not have guessed they'd have that in common. And now he was curious if she'd lain awake fantasizing about what might have happened. He sure the hell had.

A blush stained her cheeks. "Shut up and stop reading into everything I'm saying."

"Is that what I'm doing?"

The concept shouldn't have made him smile, but she seemed so flustered. He liked knowing that she'd been affected by what had happened in his workshop, especially since he'd have sworn she'd backed off because she had little interest in exploring the attraction between them.

Maybe she was more interested than he'd assumed.

She groaned. "Please tell me you didn't really seek me out to issue the third degree."

"No. My apologies if that's how it came across." He could circle back to their attraction and the potential for more kissing experiments later. "I have a list of candidates from the nanny service. I wanted to see when you might be available to discuss them."

"Now," she shot back. "No time like the present. The baby has about ten more minutes on this side and then I have to switch, so I'm stuck for the duration."

"Stuck?"

"Yeah, it's not like I can drive to the store in my current state," she explained wryly. "It's a necessary part of the job that you have to stay pretty much parked in one spot. I had to learn the hard way to always go to the bathroom first. It's not a big deal. You get used to it and, honestly, I use the downtime to kind of Zen out."

He'd never considered that she was essentially trapped while breast-feeding. But it wasn't as if she could move around, get a glass of water if she grew thirsty. The realization sat uncomfortably behind his rib cage. While he'd been obsessing over how to get her into his arms again, she'd been quietly taking care of his son without any thought to her own comfort. "What can I get for you? Some tea? A pillow?"

What else did nursing women need? He'd have to do a Google search, watch some videos.

She smiled; the first one he'd gotten out of her since he'd interrupted her Zen. "Thanks, I'm okay. I learned to get all that stuff before starting, too."

It was a conviction of his gender that he'd never even contemplated any of this. Maybe even a conviction of his parenting skills. There was no excuse for him having left her to her own devices as she did something as sacred and necessary as feeding his son. "From now on, I want to be in the room when you feed Conner."

"What? Why?" Suspiciously, she eyed him.

"I simply wish to support you in the one aspect of Conner's care I can't control. If you're stuck, then I should be, too."

"Oh. That's...unexpected."

"I'm not a beast all the time." Only when it mattered.

She actually laughed at that. "I never said you were. Thank you. It's really not necessary for you to hang out with me. It'll probably be pretty boring."

"Conner is my son. You're my wife. I'm nothing if not avidly interested in both of you."

That seemed to set her back and she stared at him for a long moment. "I'm definitely not used to a man who's so forthcoming."

What kind of men did she normally surround herself with? Discomfort ruffled the hairs on the back of his neck. That was a subject best left unexplored.

"Find better people to associate with," he advised her brusquely. *Now* it was time to move on. "I've reviewed the list of nannies. There are four that stand out. I'd like your opinion on them."

"Sure."

She casually popped Conner's mouth from her nipple with a finger and rolled him back on the nursing pillow to adjust her bra cup. Then she unhooked the other side, peeling it away from her breast without seeming to notice that a man was in the room avidly attempting to pretend she hadn't just bared herself.

Perhaps demanding to be present every time she fed Conner wasn't such a bright idea. He shifted, but there was no comfortable spot when sporting an erection that never should have happened. He hated that he couldn't control it, hated how wrong it felt and hated that he couldn't enjoy the sight of his wife's body like a normal husband.

But he couldn't, not without infringing on her insistence that getting involved was a bad idea. And neither could he take back his insistence on supporting her, especially given that he hadn't hired a nanny yet. Until then, he'd suffer in the trap of his own making.

"Why don't you read me the résumés?" she suggested.

He blinked. Yes. Good plan. "Be right back."

He dashed to his room and grabbed his tablet from

the bedside table, booting up the device on his way back to the solarium. By the time he hit the west wing of the house, he had his email client up and the list on the screen.

McKenna hadn't moved from her spot in the chair by the window. Sunlight spilled in through the glass, highlighting her dark hair like a corona. With Conner tucked in close, she was absolutely the most beautiful woman he'd ever seen.

There came the *thwack* to his chest, true to form.

He had to fix that. It was a problem he couldn't deconstruct and then rebuild. All he could think about was kissing her again and not stopping. He liked this attraction between them. When had he lost all his brain cells?

"I, um, have the list," he announced unnecessarily, but she just nodded and didn't call him on his idiocy.

Clearing his throat, he read through the credentials of the four candidates he'd selected from the list of twenty. She interrupted every so often to clarify a point, ask him to repeat a section or remind her of a detail from a previous candidate. When he finished, he lowered the tablet and cocked his head. "What do you think?"

"I like number three the best," she announced immediately. "Shelly. Her phrasing gave me a comfort level that she wasn't trying to pad her experience with a lot of flowery words. She's the only one who's cared for two different infants with formula allergies. And I'll admit an age prejudice. She's two years older than the others. When it comes to caring for my—your—son, that's no small thing."

The slip hung in the air, daring him to comment on it. He should. Conner was her son in only one sense of the word. Des had ironclad documents stating such. The odds were good she hadn't forgotten that, not when Des was holding back the divorce as a guarantee she'd stay.

McKenna wasn't confused about her role here. Not at all. She'd been the one to back off in his workshop, citing her belief that getting involved wasn't a good plan.

Maybe *Desmond* needed the reminder about her role.

He chose to let the slip go by without comment and she didn't miss it. Her brows drew together. "I want the best for Conner, too, of course. I assume you know that or you wouldn't have asked my opinion."

Actually he hadn't considered that. At all. Wanting the best for the baby implied emotional attachment, which was the opposite of what he'd expected to happen here. She'd completely misinterpreted his request for her help and he'd completely missed that she'd developed a bond with the baby.

Taking a seat on the long leather couch facing the window, he laid the tablet to the side as he processed.

"I asked you to help select the nanny because I assumed you would want to ensure I picked someone suited to helping you wean. So you could leave with a clean slate."

Something akin to pain flashed across her face. "Yes, I have an interest in that, too. But that's the point. This woman is my replacement. I want it to be the right person to raise Connor."

"I will raise Conner," he corrected somewhat ferociously. He had a fierce need for his son and he wasn't shy about it.

"Well, of course, but he needs a female influence. Someone who can be nurturing and kiss his boo-boos when he falls down." She swept him with a once-over that she probably didn't mean to be provocative but was nonetheless. "Somehow I don't see you filling that role."

"Because I'm male?"

Sexist, definitely. But even worse, he wasn't sure she

was wrong. He didn't see himself as nurturing in the slightest. The relationship he envisioned with Conner would be of the mind as they discussed the philosophy of physics and argued theories or studied ancient history together. He'd never once thought he'd be the one sticking Band-Aids on his son's knees, though all of his research showed Conner would need that.

"No, because you're you," she countered without heat. "It has nothing to do with being male. I've seen lots of men be single fathers for one reason or another, but they were more...adaptable to the requirements. You're outsourcing the job of mom and I want to get the right person for that, so you can go back to hiding in your workshop."

"I don't—" *Hide.* Except he did and the fact that she'd clued in to that bothered him. How did she read him so well? Better still, she'd noticed a gap in Desmond's parenting experience and brought it to the forefront. "Tell me more about child rearing in your community."

"Really?" She glanced up, her confusion evident. "That doesn't seem like your cup of tea."

On that, she *was* wrong. "On the contrary. I have an interest in ensuring Conner grows into a happy, healthy adult. I have a job, too, albeit not the bandager of knees apparently."

She stuck her tongue out at him and the sight of it shouldn't have been as suggestive as it was, but instantly he recalled the feel of it, exploratory and hot, against his. She'd kissed him eagerly, as if she'd been waiting for him to breech that wall between them. He couldn't stop himself from wanting her hands on him again.

Crossing his legs, he tried to hide the worst of the tenting in his pants but he was pretty sure that was impossible when he'd just created a mountain in his lap. What was he supposed to do to tamp down this visceral reaction he always had to McKenna?

"I'm not saying you can't," she said, thankfully oblivious to Des's inability to stop reacting like a horny teenager whenever she breathed too hard. "Just that you're not going to be the first person he thinks of running to when he's bleeding and hurt. That's what I notice when thinking about how the families at home raise babies. Mothers and fathers alike read to their kids at night before bed. Get up with them when they have nightmares and soothe them back to sleep. Feeding, changing wet sheets, looking for lost stuffed animals. The person who demonstrates the most love, tolerance and patience will be who he comes to in crisis. And there are a lot of crises for children."

As she'd talked, her hand drifted over Conner's head, absently stroking his fine baby hair. Des doubted she'd even noticed that her fingers hadn't stopped moving, even after her voice stopped. McKenna was natural at nurturing, did it without thought. Did she realize that?

"And you assume the nanny will be that person." All at once, he couldn't imagine anyone other than McKenna being that person. He tried transposing one of the women on his list into his wife's spot on the chair, bottle in hand, and it refused to materialize.

That was...disturbing. And unexpected.

She shrugged. "Maybe I'm wrong. In that case, you tell me which nanny candidate you like the best and your criteria for choosing."

No. He was done with this discussion. She'd challenged a lot of his assumptions and brought up things he'd not examined. He needed time to acclimate to all of this new information.

But he couldn't leave. McKenna was still breast-feeding. And trapped. That meant he was, too, because he'd given his word. Suddenly his skin felt too tight as the first wave of what might be a panic attack stole over him. God, he hadn't had one of those in years, usually because he avoided all of his triggers.

"Desmond." McKenna's strong voice washed over him, filtering through the anxiety in a flash.

He pried open his eyelids, which he hadn't even realized he'd closed, to see her watching him with concern flitting across her expression. She'd tucked her clothes back into place and cradled Conner in her arms as he waved a hand in a circle, content after his feeding.

"Would you like to hold him?" she offered casually, as if she hadn't noticed he'd slid into his own head. But he didn't believe for a second she'd missed it. Neither did he mistake her offer as anything other than an intervention. She'd noticed he was troubled and sought to help him.

It worked. Somehow. As she set the nursing pillow aside and crossed the room, his body cooled and settled. Conner nestled into Des's arms and he definitely didn't need any more information to know that he loved his son. The emotion bled through him, a balm to his frazzled nerves.

Yes. This part wasn't in question. He'd wanted a baby because he'd needed this connection. From the first moment Lacey had announced that she was pregnant, his heart had instantly been engaged with the idea of a child. A baby wouldn't know that Des stumbled over things normal people did without question. His son would love him even after realizing his father hated crowds and preferred to be alone.

"I want you to come to me for bandages," he murmured softly, but McKenna heard him anyway. Her hand drifted to his shoulder, gentle and warm, and that felt right, too.

"Then he will," she promised. "I didn't mean to speak out of turn."

"No. You just caused me to think about aspects of being a single father that I previously hadn't." Maybe he didn't want a nanny. It wasn't like he needed to work to provide for his son. If Des took off a year, even two, who would care?

Well, he would. His brain did not stop creating, whether he wished it to or not. Putting the pieces together of what he saw was merely a defense mechanism designed to empty his mind. But he didn't have to be a full-time inventor or even sell anything he created, which meant no business trips to the manufacturer's locations. Nothing to distract him from being a father.

It could just be Des and Conner. Father and son. No nanny needed.

McKenna smiled. "I'm glad. The secret to being a great father is that there is no secret. All you have to do is love them. And there's nothing wrong with picking a nanny who's more in the background. As long as she can work with Conner's formula allergy, I think that's the most important thing."

All at once the reality of the situation crashed through his bubble of contentment. If he didn't hire a nanny, what did that mean for McKenna and weaning? Could *he* be the one who helped her through that? Would she even accept that?

He'd never failed to master a concept in his life. If he studied up on it, surely he could fare as well as a nanny. And then, as a bonus, working together would give him more of an opportunity to be around her. Feel out what was happening between them and his odd, disconcerting urge to bury himself inside her and never emerge.

Hiring a nanny would only impede that process.

But he couldn't tell McKenna. Not yet. First he had to figure out how to convince her it was the right decision.

While Des had already done a good bit of research on Conner's formula allergy, he hadn't spent any effort on how to transition from breast-feeding to something else because it hadn't mattered yet. Now it did.

From the moment he woke up the next day until well after lunch, he studied. With way too many videos starring breast-feeding women on a continual loop in his head, he let it go for the day and took a shower.

Des's bedroom resembled a small fortress. By design. When he'd bought the house, he'd cared mostly about its proximity to other people. Namely that they were as far away as they could be. The two-hundred-acre property guaranteed that, and the forest of trees and wild undergrowth surrounding the main house shielded him from unwanted trespassers. But just to make sure, he'd installed a twelve-foot concrete wall around the grounds.

He'd stopped short at a pack of Dobermans to roam the property. Overkill. And thus far McKenna had been his only guest, so he'd accomplished his goal of cutting himself off from those who didn't tolerate his eccentricities. For an additional escape, he'd created a bedroom retreat that rivaled the poshest resorts complete with a pop-up TV, a large, oval spa tub in the cavernous bathroom and a small sitting area in the garden outside a set of French doors.

Shame he rarely spent time here, often napping in his workshop on the single bed he'd eventually had delivered when he'd fallen asleep at his desk for the tenth time. The suite was a place to hold his clothes and store his shampoo, but that was it. The workshop was his home.

Maybe not so much anymore if he didn't hire a nanny.

The concept of losing his sanctuary filled him with a black soup of nerves. But, as he continually told himself, he wasn't losing his workshop. Just committing to spend less time hiding and more time with the family he was creating with his son.

To that end, he had to actually do that. Throwing on some clothes, he went in search of his son. He found both the baby and McKenna in the nursery. She held Conner upright in her lap as she read him a chunky board book.

He cleared his throat. "Thanks for watching him while I was busy."

"You're welcome." Her slightly cocked eyebrow had a saucy bent to it, like she questioned why he was being pleasant.

McKenna wore a dress today. A rarity. Usually she had on capri pants and a short-sleeved shirt or yoga pants and a tunic. The dress showed off her feminine curves in a way he fully appreciated.

Then she smiled at Conner as he waved a chubby fist in a circle, and the desire Des had no ability to keep in check roared through his chest like a freight train. Coupled with everything else, it was nearly enough to put him over the edge.

"Did you need something?" she asked before he'd regained his sanity.

"Do I have to need something to spend time with my son?"

To her credit, she didn't flinch at his less than civil tone. "Wanting to spend time with your son is a need. There's nothing wrong with claiming it as such, especially if I'm in the way."

She levered herself out of the chair and plopped Conner into his arms, then turned, clearly about to leave the room, which had not been his intent at all.

"Wait," he called out awkwardly as Conner started fussing.

McKenna glanced back over her shoulder. "You'll be fine. He just ate not too long ago, so he might be ready for a diaper change."

"I want you to stay," he ground out. This was not one of his more stellar examples of communicating with other people.

"Why?" She seemed genuinely perplexed, like she had no concept of how she made the room brighter by being in it. Why *wouldn't* he want her to stay? "I'm just the buffet."

"That's so far from the truth," he shot back and then registered that he'd meant it.

She was more than just a means to an end. McKenna was his wife. Against everything he'd expected when he'd convinced her to come home with him from the hospital, she'd begun to matter.

"I like you," he said, marking the first time he could recall saying anything resembling that out loud to anyone. Not even Lacey.

It was an event.

McKenna was no longer just his son's surrogate mother, and Des didn't have a good foundation for managing that.

"Yes, I got that impression the other day in your workshop," she replied blithely with an ironic smile. "I hope you aren't angling for a repeat."

Of the kiss? What if he was?

No better way to take control than to lay out exactly what was on his mind. Besides, she'd seemed rather impressed with his tendency to be forthcoming. Sometimes he had no filter owing to his lack of social niceties and other times because he genuinely didn't see the point in filtering. People could take him or leave him and usually he preferred the latter.

Except with McKenna.

And she was still edging toward the door.

"McKenna." She froze. He pressed the advantage. "Stay. We live in the same house and share a son. I like your company. Unless the reverse isn't true?"

"What, are you asking me if I like hanging around with you?" She leaned against the open door as she surveyed him. "I basically spend my days feeding your son. Adult conversation is high on my list of things I look forward to."

Obviously she viewed herself as the milk supply and he'd done nothing to counter that. Perhaps it was time to change their association in her mind. In both their minds. She was a person with her own interests, dreams and opinions, some of which he'd already glimpsed, but not nearly enough.

"Then there's no reason for you to leave." Satisfied that he'd navigated this small blip, he nodded to the chair she'd recently vacated. "Sit while I change Conner's diaper. Tell me something about you that I don't know."

"You want me to provide entertainment for you?" The quirk of her mouth said she found the concept amusing but she sat in the chair as he'd asked.

"No. Insight." The more he knew about her, the more information he had at his disposal to figure out how to exorcise her from his consciousness. But even that excuse was starting to fall short.

He just wanted to know her. Period.

"I like cotton candy, thunderstorms and books about dogs. That kind of thing?" At his nod, she laughed. "I feel like I'm on a date."

Instantly a dozen different scenarios sprang to his

mind, scenes where he romanced what he wanted out of McKenna, held her hand as he led her along a rain-soaked trail through the woods. Pressed her against a tree as he fed her cotton candy from his fingers, then kissed her to treat them both to the taste of sweetness mixed with the fire that laced their electric attraction.

He was going about his problem solving in the wrong way. If he wanted insight, a next kiss, to spend time with McKenna, "hanging out" wasn't going to cut it. He needed to ask her on a date.

Five

McKenna did not like the look on Desmond's face. Or rather, she liked it a whole hell of a lot and shouldn't.

The second the word *date* had come out of her stupid mouth, something heated and thoroughly intrigued popped into his gaze and hadn't fled in over a minute.

It was a long minute, too, as he watched her without apology, contemplating. She could almost see the gears turning in his head and one of Desmond's sexiest qualities was his mind. She'd gone to college with a lot of smart people, but Desmond's brain was wired so differently, evidenced by the fascinating way he presented thoughts and concepts, drew conclusions. Threw out unexpected comments such as *I like you.*

Sometimes she wondered if he did stuff like that as a test. To see what she'd do. But she had no rubric for the grading system and therefore no way of knowing if she'd passed or not. Or whether she wanted to pass.

She and Desmond weren't supposed to become friends. Or anything else.

"We never finished our nanny discussion," she blurted out lamely, but they needed to get on to an innocuous topic. Now.

She'd grown uncomfortably aware that Desmond's hair was wet, probably because he'd come straight from the shower. It was slicked back from his forehead as it always was and hung down around his collar in solid, dark chunks. Wet, it was darker, almost black, and gave his devastating looks a wicked edge she couldn't ignore. Neither could she stop thinking about Desmond wet. And naked.

"We didn't," he allowed. "I'd like to. Another time. I have another subject of importance. Have dinner with me tonight."

She nearly choked on her gasp of surprise and the sound upset Conner, who started to cry. Desmond rocked him back and forth but his gaze never left hers.

"As in a date?" she managed to ask.

Stupid mouth. Why had she even mentioned that word? Because she'd never quite gotten that kiss out of her head, of course. She fantasized about a repeat pretty much 24/7, so no wonder she'd slipped. A smart guy like him had no problem picking up on the fact that she'd *said* it wasn't a good idea to get involved, but that didn't mean she had the ability to turn off her fascination with him.

"As in dinner. I'd like to thank you for what you've done for Conner. And for me." His gentle rocking soothed Conner into a doze, his sweet face nestled against Desmond's chest. "You're a guest. I haven't welcomed you as one."

Oh. That was a different story. Slightly. It still sounded like all the trappings of a date without slapping the label on it. "Would it just be me and you? What about Conner? Right now, we're it as far as a caregiver goes."

"Mrs. Elliot will fill in for a few hours."

He had an answer to everything, didn't he? Desperately, she cast about for a plausible reason to refuse. Except, she wanted to have dinner with Desmond. Fiercely. And have it be every bit a date, with all the long, delicious glances over dessert as anticipation coiled in her belly…

Bad, bad idea.

"I don't have anything to wear."

The protest died in her throat as he swept her with a look that could have melted the habit off of a nun. "I have yet to see you in clothing that I did not think looked spectacular on you. Wear anything. Or nothing. I'm not particular."

The shiver his suggestion unleashed shouldn't have gone so deep into her skin. It was the most flirtatious thing he'd ever said. That any man had dared to say to her. She shouldn't like it so much, but all at once, the muddle he was making of her request to stay uninvolved put her in a dangerous mood.

"I'd love to see the look on your face if I took that dare."

One eyebrow cocked at a quizzical angle. "It wasn't a dare. I merely sought to make you more comfortable about the circumstances. If you want to see my expression once you grant me the privilege of seeing you naked, my calendar is completely clear for the evening."

Somehow that got a laugh out of her. Mostly because she had a feeling he wasn't kidding. There was something so affecting about knowing exactly where she stood with him. He liked her. He wanted to see her naked. No guessing.

But he also wanted to divorce her. The contradictions were dizzying.

"What if I say yes? Are you expecting sex as payback for dinner?"

"No. I'm expecting you to eat as payback for putting food in front of you. Though, again…if you want sex to be a part of the evening, my calendar is still open."

She shut her eyes for a beat. Why was she so surprised he'd be gentlemanly about it, putting all the balls in her court? "I don't."

She did.

Oh, God, did she want sex to be a part of her relationship with Desmond. The way he communicated with his hands during a simple kiss had kept her awake and feverish far longer than it should have. But she couldn't help imaging how much hotter those hands could be with no barriers between them.

What was wrong with her? She and Desmond had the most dysfunctional marriage on the planet and sex would only complicate everything. And then what would happen? She'd end up divorced and in medical school. Exactly as she'd planned.

She blinked. "I'll have dinner with you."

And maybe sex would be on the menu, after all. What did she have to lose besides this achy, vibrating tension between her and the man with the keys to her future?

McKenna pulled out her best dress from the back of the giant closet. Everything at Desmond's house was huge, including him. His presence dominated every inch of his realm. There was literally nowhere she could go to escape his effect on her, particularly not her bedroom.

He'd become a permanent fixture when she breast-fed, which she appreciated more than she'd have expected.

But the middle-of-the-night visits were hard to take, when she was semiconscious and Desmond wore drawstring lounge pants and a white T-shirt that showcased surprisingly broad shoulders.

It seemed natural for him to be in her bedroom. It was almost hard to watch him leave when she had to go back to her cold bed alone. That had never bothered her before. But she'd never experienced such a magnetic draw to a man before either.

And in ten minutes they were going to have dinner in what she definitely considered a date. As long as everyone understood that getting involved only worked for the short term. Surely that was Desmond's thought, too.

Nervous all at once, McKenna twirled in front of the oval cheval glass in the corner of her room. She'd never had a full-length mirror before and loved it. When she left, she'd miss that, plus a lot of the other luxuries strewed throughout the mansion, especially the indoor pool.

Of course she had to actually leave before she could miss them.

The mirror reflected a woman who looked the best she could. Her hair was low maintenance, wash and go as soon as it was dry, but she'd given it extra help with a blow-dryer a few minutes ago. No makeup, thank God, because who wanted to sit around with goop on their face? The dress fit her angular body well, except for her bust line. The fabric hugged her cleavage, smooshing it prominently high and out. Only her maternity clothes accommodated her enormous boobs, but without the baby bump, she might as well wear a potato sack on her date with Desmond. Not happening. Besides, he'd seen her breasts lots of times. No reason to hide them.

When she descended the main staircase to the ground

floor, Desmond was waiting for her at the bottom. His gaze locked onto her, hot and appreciative, sending little quakes through her core that put a whole new spin on the concept of long, delicious glances.

"Conner is settled with Mrs. Elliot and a bottle of breast milk," he informed her casually, as if he hadn't just undressed her with his eyes. "Shall we?"

He gestured with his hand toward the dining room, signaling her to walk with him. Nerves and a whole lot of zingy sparks shot around under her skin, making her jumpy. The dining room conformed to the rest of the house: cavernous, a little formal and thoroughly drenched with Desmond.

During the first course of garden salad, served by the invisible staff Mrs. Elliot managed, Desmond said, "Tell me about being part of a cooperative community."

"What? All of it?"

"Sure. Whatever you want to tell me. I imagine it shaped you in many invisible ways. I'm curious."

She swallowed. This was definitely not first-date material. It was far deeper, opening aspects of her soul she wasn't sure she wanted on display. "I don't know. I don't sit around and think about my upbringing."

Except she did sometimes. Being part of a closed, united community had a lot of pluses, but losing her grandfather hadn't been one of them. It *had* shaped her. And, based on his comment, Desmond had already figured that out.

"But it matters," he said quietly, and it wasn't a question.

His insight bothered her. She forked up a bite of lettuce and tomato to stall but his piercing gaze penetrated her anyway. "Well, yeah. Of course."

"Did it contribute to your decision to be my surrogate?"

"My background has everything to do with why I'm Conner's mother," she told him firmly. "I was raised to believe that we each have a purpose in life. I discovered early on that mine is to help people when they're hurting. You wanted a baby really badly and I had the power to give you the family you wished for. It was a no-brainer."

"Thank you," he said simply. "Conner means more to me than anything else I've ever created. I would not have him without you."

The sincerity in his voice choked her up. Why, she couldn't say. She shouldn't be privy to any of this.

McKenna blinked back the sudden moisture in her eyes, mystified why it meant so much to her that she shared something so deeply personal with Desmond.

He fell silent, watching her as the staff cleared the salad plates and replaced them with the main course of locally fished salmon and asparagus. But instead of picking up his fork to dig in, he cocked his head. "Perhaps you'd be interested in taking a role in Conner's life on a longer term basis."

"What?" Her own fork clattered to her plate. "What are you talking about? That's not the deal."

It couldn't be the deal. What did he mean? Like, picking Conner up from school or taking him to the zoo occasionally? She couldn't do that. Didn't Desmond know how hard it already was to contemplate leaving? It was easier to not have contact. That's what she'd been counting on.

"No, it's not." Steadily, he measured his words as he spoke. "But you care about Conner already. I can see it in your face when you hold him. There's no reason we can't discuss a different arrangement."

Still reeling, she gaped at him. Was he insane? "I can't

do that. You shouldn't want me to do that. What about when he starts asking questions about who I am? I won't lie. And then he'll wonder why I don't live with you and be a real mother."

It would be a disaster. And, of course, Conner might still have those same questions, but she'd much rather let Desmond answer them than be put on the hot seat herself. As a surrogate, none of this should have ever been presented to her and the unfairness of it hammered at her heart.

She wasn't mother material. The first criterion was wanting to be one and she didn't. Or rather, she didn't have the luxury of wanting to be one, which wasn't the same thing, as she'd only just come to realize. It was be a doctor or be a mother. Period. And she'd made her choice so long ago that she'd reconciled it in her mind.

Until now.

The salmon dried up in her mouth as she wrestled with the impossibility of Desmond's suggestion. With the fact that her decisions weren't as cut-and-dried as she'd have once claimed.

She did care for Conner. So much so that Desmond had noticed.

Well, it didn't matter. She cared about the baby for the same reasons she wanted to be a doctor; she genuinely wanted to help Conner. The soul-deep need to fix what was wrong came so naturally that she couldn't remember a time when she hadn't wanted to be a doctor.

Besides, as soon as Desmond signed the divorce papers, the custody agreement would go into effect and all of this would be a moot point. She was here to say a long goodbye, nothing more.

"There is a reason we can't discuss this," she reminded him, but her throat was so tight it was a miracle any sound came out. "You've been really clear about the fact that you don't want me involved in Conner's life."

"I didn't, no. But obviously circumstances have shifted."

"You don't like to share," she blurted, confused about the direction of the conversation. What happened to the delicious, sensual undertones she'd anticipated for their date? "Unless you've changed your mind about being the one to make all the decisions?"

"I haven't." His tone cooled considerably. "And you're right. I'm not being fair. There isn't a way to alter our agreement to permit you a role in Conner's life past the one you have currently."

A prickle walked down her spine as she watched Desmond shut down. Their date disintegrated into a long, uncomfortable silence as she grappled to understand what had just happened. They both ate but the stilted vibe turned everything unpleasant.

"I take it your calendar isn't so clear anymore," she muttered as the staff unobtrusively removed the dinner dishes. Hers was embarrassingly unfinished, with half the salmon lying forlornly near the edge of the plate, but she'd lost her appetite.

He glanced up. "My interest in you hasn't changed, if that's what you mean. But I sense the timing is not the best."

"Yeah. That."

It had seemed so easy to imagine that they'd have some hot sex and then she'd get her divorce at some point in the future so she could leave.

But Desmond had just dropped a whole lot of reality in her lap. He had all the control and would never give up any. The thought of getting involved with someone who refused to allow her choices didn't sit well.

Rubbing at his beard, Desmond frowned. "I've angered you."

"No." Not really. He had been completely transparent from the first and she'd ignored all the warning signs that had been screaming at her to stay far away from the father of her baby. "I...just need some air."

She excused herself and went to her room to get some sleep before the sole source of her uneasiness visited her room for Conner's midnight feeding. The sooner he hired a nanny, the better.

Once again, McKenna had run away from him. Desmond stared out the window in Conner's nursery as he sat in the rocking chair holding his son later that night.

It was far from the first time a woman had edged for the door while in the midst of a date. But this marked a rarity in that it still bothered him hours later. How had things disintegrated so quickly? First they'd been talking about McKenna's upbringing and the conversation had shifted to Conner. Why not? The baby was one of the things they had in common.

But then she'd grown upset when he'd mentioned that she might extend her role, maybe spending time with their son on a regular basis. It seemed a simple enough concept, but clearly McKenna wished to keep their agreement as it was. Nor did she want to explore their attraction.

Which was the root of the problem—he did and apparently she'd clued in far too fast that he didn't have a charming personality at his disposal to woo a woman into his bed. So he'd have to be a little more inventive than the average Joe, clearly.

He dissected their dialogue, trying to pinpoint where he'd messed up.

This had been a problem his whole life. Nothing ever unfolded the way he'd constructed it in his mind, not when people were involved. Metal parts and computer programs always came together exactly as he intended. The final creation resembled the one he'd imagined. Always. His relationship with McKenna? Not even close.

Conner circled his fist and whacked Desmond in the chest. All at once, Des had the unsettling realization that his son was a person. Unless he figured out how to relate to people, he might very well have the same issues with his child once Conner grew old enough to talk. Of course, Desmond had envisioned that the baby would love him. But years of evidence indicated otherwise.

A wash of emotion tightened his chest as he captured Conner's little fist and held it in his. When McKenna had said his son wouldn't come to him with a scraped knee, she'd meant because Desmond was difficult to relate to. Conner wouldn't naturally seek out his father.

Des had to fix his people skills if he ever hoped to forge the connections he craved.

Once Conner fell asleep, Des settled him into his crib with a silent vow that he'd never give his son a reason to run away from him. That meant he had to figure out how to entice his mother to stay, since they likely shared similarities. The problem wheeled through his mind constantly, keeping Des from fully relaxing.

The hour of sleep he got before Conner woke him for his midnight feeding didn't put him in any better frame of mind. McKenna was always so much more beautiful in the semidarkness, too.

She answered her door wearing her virginal white robe that left everything to the imagination and an expression that could have frozen lava.

Usually her naturally friendly personality was in place

no matter the time or circumstance. Was she still upset about dinner? She'd said she wasn't angry. Had that been one of those times when a woman was less than forthcoming and Des should have figured out that she meant the opposite of what she'd said?

He hated being forced to read between the lines. "Conner is ready for you."

That could have come out with less of a growl. But when uncertain, he tended to retreat behind his walls. He couldn't afford to do so tonight, and cursed himself for being such a brute.

"I assumed so."

She reached out and took the baby from his arms, brushing her fingers across Desmond's chest. The T-shirt he wore provided little barrier from the thrill of her touch, which seemed constant regardless of whether things were prickly between them.

The familiar rush of awareness didn't diminish just because McKenna wasn't speaking to him. His conscience poked at him. If he wanted to change the status quo, this was a great opportunity for him to take the initiative.

"I'm, uh, sorry about earlier," he offered cautiously as she settled into the recliner with Conner. "I did not intend for dinner to end on such a bad note."

"I know." The barest hint of a smile turned up the edges of her mouth. It wasn't much, but it felt like a lot.

Instead of letting her handle her own logistics, he picked up the nursing pillow from the floor and arranged it in her lap the way he'd seen her do a dozen times. Then he helped her get Conner situated, a trick and a half since the baby already knew what was coming and had squirmed into place against McKenna's covered bosom. There wasn't enough room for two sets of hands, a baby and the enormous sensual pull that seemed constantly coiled between Desmond and McKenna. But he stuck it out and ignored the ache that sprang up at the sight of his son and wife together in the most elemental scene a man could have the privilege to witness.

And therein lay part of his confusion and consternation. His attraction to McKenna had a thread running through it that was inexorably due to the fact that she was Conner's mother. It was unexpected. Powerful. Impossible to mistake. What was he supposed to do with that?

"I'm sorry, too," she said after the longest pause.

His gaze flew to hers. "For what? I'm the one who overstepped at dinner."

"No, you didn't. It was very generous of you to offer to reexamine the agreement. I know your heart was in the right place. I...freaked out and made it weird."

That set him back for a moment. Emotional decisions weren't in his wheelhouse. Or were they? "Only because I suggested something that had no logical possibility. It was a mistake."

One borne out of his visceral need to connect and he'd bungled it.

"On that we agree." She tipped her head back against the recliner, letting her eyes flutter closed. "It would be too hard, Desmond. I hope you understand that."

All at once, he had an inkling of what she meant. McKenna cared for Conner. He hadn't gotten that part wrong, though he'd questioned what he'd seen after their discussion, assuming he'd completely misinterpreted the expression that always stole over her face when she held him. "Hard because you're giving up a relationship with your son?"

Her misty smile was a little wider this time. "It shouldn't be. I never would have thought twice about it if you hadn't asked me to breast-feed. Or, at least, I don't think I would have. Who can say at this point?"

Her pain convicted him, winnowing through his pores as easily as if he'd poured it down his throat. He'd changed the dynamic and forced her to help, with no thought to the resulting emotional turmoil he'd be causing her. Or himself.

The empathy he'd always felt for other people's strongest emotions amplified under his own unease. *Why* did he have to experience feelings so strongly? It was exactly why he stayed away from people. But he couldn't have stayed away from McKenna short of being chained in the basement.

"I didn't realize," he finally ground out through clenched teeth as he battled to get the clash of emotion gripping his chest to ease. She hurt. Therefore, he did, too. "I'm sorry."

"I made the choice." She shrugged. "And it was the right one. What would have happened to Conner if I wasn't here to feed him? It's ghastly to even consider. So it's a done deal. The only thing we can do at this point is move forward. Hire a nanny who can help us figure out the options so I can leave."

If he hadn't been paying such close attention to her, he might have missed the desolate note in her voice. But all at once he had the distinct impression she wasn't in such a hurry to leave as she had been.

Also a benefit of being so closely tuned in to one another. He could tell what she was feeling as clearly as if she'd hung a sign around her neck.

And he had to admit that he wasn't in such a hurry for her to go either. He should be. She stirred him in ways that made him uncomfortable. But she stirred him in ways that thrilled him, too. The wonder of that kept him engaged. If he was this attuned to her now, he could only image how much more strongly they might connect in the throes of pleasure.

"I've been doing some research into formula allergies," he said casually. "It's very difficult to say how Conner will stack up against the data. He may not wean for six months."

"I know." She glanced up at Des, her expression indecipherable. "I've looked into it, as well. I may be here until he's on solid food."

"Would that be so bad?" It was a bold question and, judging by the long, heavy silence, she didn't miss the significance of it. They were talking about further alterations to the agreement.

She heaved a deep breath. "Only because it puts my goals on hold even longer."

Not because she'd be stuck here with him. Not because she didn't like taking care of Conner. More had changed than just the circumstances. But how much? Enough that she might reevaluate the complications standing between them?

He couldn't barrel ahead as he'd half planned. As his body screamed for him to. If he didn't want to ruin things between them, he had to take his time. Romance her until she was hot and breathless.

He chewed on the idea until the next morning. During Conner's midmorning nap, Des considered how to court his wife. The techniques felt fake and disingenuous, like he'd have to become someone else to simply hold a conversation with a normal person.

But his wife and son weren't normal people. He loved Conner, and McKenna… Well, he couldn't say for sure how he felt about her, but it wasn't lukewarm by any stretch. She did matter, as he'd told her. The only piece of advice that he'd gleaned from all of his research on talking to people was to engage McKenna at her level of interest.

McKenna wanted to go to medical school and he'd held her back thus far. It was time to rectify that to the best of his ability.

Six

When McKenna had too much rattling around in her brain, she liked to swim. Lately she'd been spending several hours a day at the pool as she tried to get her mind off the constant turmoil under her skin.

Not only had she let herself start to care about Conner, Desmond had noticed. Noticed and commented. That made it real.

She hated the quandary. Conner couldn't be her son and she'd walked into this agreement willingly. Sure she'd known it would be difficult to give up the baby at the hospital, but she'd done it, even though it had been harder than she'd ever imagined. She'd reconciled the loss by envisioning the family Desmond would create for himself, believing that as time went on, the regret would fade.

None of that had happened. Desmond had taken her life over by storm and, instead of moving on, she'd chosen to be in the position of caring for her son day in, day out…only to have to eventually give him up again. Each additional day she stayed in this house meant one more chink in her heart. And she'd known for a while that Desmond would eventually bring up the fact that his original three-month proposal was likely dead in the water.

Being stuck in this nebulous role of mother and not mother was killing her.

How was she going to manage the mess she was making of this?

Swimming helped. But not much. Especially when she broke the surface of the water to see Desmond sitting on one of the lounge chairs, gorgeous and intense and untouchable. Her pulse stumbled and the perfect temperature of the pool rose a few degrees.

She hadn't seen him since last night. Conner had thankfully dropped one of the nighttime feedings, but showed no signs of forgetting about the remaining one, which meant a tension-filled encounter with Desmond lay in store for her like clockwork. She wished she could say she'd shut down his advances and then dismissed him from her mind.

Not so much. As if the thought of leaving Conner behind wasn't difficult enough, she couldn't get his father out from under her skin either. Late at night there were fewer barriers somehow. The dark created an oasis where anything was possible and nothing bad could touch the three of them.

Then when the sun rose she remembered all the reasons she couldn't indulge in the sizzle that sprang up anytime Desmond entered a room.

The echoing pool area amplified the undercurrents between them in spades.

"Conner is down for his nap," he announced—unnecessarily since McKenna knew the baby's schedule well.

"And that seemed like a good opportunity to tell me you hired a nanny?" she suggested hopefully.

"Not yet."

Of course not. What fun would that be? His highness liked to have control and wield his power as he saw fit.

And now she felt petulant and ungrateful. The man was treating *her* like royalty, not acting like he expected everyone to kowtow to his bidding. Desmond wished to keep an iron fist around all of the decisions regarding his son. It wasn't a crime and it was certainly his right. Some people might simply call it being protective.

"You could have flagged me down if you needed to talk," she murmured.

Like the last time he'd cornered her here, he wasn't dressed for swimming. In fact, she'd never seen him in anything but pants and a shirt.

The long look he shot her shouldn't have put so much heat in her blood. She was suddenly very aware that the swimsuit she wore might have been considered modest on most women, but on the body of one who was breast-feeding, it became more of a boob showcase starring pointy, chilled nipples.

Some of that might be the fault of Desmond and his hot-eyed gaze that never failed to make her feel both sexy and appreciated.

"I didn't want to bother you," he said with a shake of his head far past the time when it would have been appropriate to respond.

Too late for that. "But now that I know you're here, it's okay?"

He blinked. "I can come back."

God, sometimes he was so adorable. Why was that such a thing? She'd never met anyone quite like Desmond Pierce and she was pretty sure that was the reason she couldn't stop thinking about him, despite the surety that getting involved would be the worst idea ever.

"I'm just kidding." She kicked to the edge of the pool and rested her arms on the flagstone lip surrounding the water, mostly so the whole of her body was hidden from his too sharp gaze. "You should swim sometime."

"Is that an invitation?" he asked with raised eyebrows…and there came more of the heat that turned the whole exchange into a double entendre. Everything he said lately seemed centered on sex, probably because it was on both their minds constantly.

Cursing her stupid mouth, she shut her eyes for a beat. What was wrong with her that she hadn't seen that coming?

"I thought we covered that. We have too many complications to get involved."

"I am referring to swimming. Only."

Yeah, right. All sorts of non-swimming-related things that could happen in a private area when two people were already nearly undressed shimmered in the atmosphere between them.

"You and I both know you aren't. So save it," she advised.

His head cocked to the side in the way she'd come to understand meant he was about to throw her into a tailspin. "This may surprise you, but I genuinely want to spend time with you."

Yep. Tailspin. "I don't know what to do with that."

"Spend time with me," he suggested wryly. "To that end, I have a surprise for you. I registered you for a couple of online classes that will count toward your medical degree."

"You did what?"

"I thought you might enjoy having something adult

to do since you mentioned that you're bored frequently. It's a gift."

This was definitely one of those times when she couldn't remember why it was a bad idea to get involved with him. No one had ever done something like that for her and it speared her right where it counted. Dumbstruck, she stared at him.

How dare he do something so generous and kindhearted when she had nothing she could do in return to thank him? "I can't accept."

"Why not?"

Argh. Because…of some reason that she couldn't put her finger on. But it felt like she should refuse. "I can't take classes that count toward my course work online. Medical school is about hands-on experience and labs. Working toward residency."

"I am aware. I reviewed the requirements and then called the dean at Oregon Health and Science University to ensure that the courses would transfer."

God, would he just stop shocking the hell out of her for a minute? "Why would you go to all that trouble, Desmond?"

"It was no trouble. You're sacrificing so much for my son. I wished to honor your goal of becoming a doctor, which I have not done a very good job of doing so far."

He'd been listening to her. And then gone out of his way to do something special for her. As gifts went, it was the best one she'd ever received.

She blew out a breath. And then another, fighting for all she was worth not to cry. It was so unexpected, so genuinely unselfish and… "Wait a minute. What's the catch?"

"McKenna, stop. There's no catch."

The raspy note in his voice flashed down her spine

and she was suddenly very glad she'd never levered herself out of the pool. He was too close as it was, too intense, too beautiful with his gaze that missed nothing, and she was very much afraid he'd just turned the tide with his imaginative present. She didn't want to find out just how deep he could take her when he finally sucked her into his orbit.

But then he rendered that point moot by crossing the few feet separating them and kneeling on the flagstone to catch her gaze as he spoke to her.

"It's a gift," he repeated and she couldn't look away. "Because I can be…hard to take. You didn't want to put off medical school, but I gave you no choice. I'm offering you a workable solution to compensate for the difficult circumstances."

That was probably the most shocking part of all.

"I'm here because I chose to be," she corrected him. *Because I continue to choose this.* It was so critical he understand he couldn't force her to do *anything*. But the rest wasn't off base. How could she say no? She couldn't. "It's a lovely thought. Thank you."

"Does that mean you're going to take the classes?"

"Yes. Of course."

Relief rushed over his expression, tripping her radar again. What was he getting out of this? "I'm cold and I'd like to go take a shower. Did you have anything else you needed to discuss? Like hiring a nanny?"

Desmond smiled. "You'll be the first to know when the nanny situation is resolved."

In addition to registering McKenna for the classes he'd selected, Desmond had also ordered her a desk, a leather chair and a top-of-the-line laptop. When they were delivered the next day, he set up everything himself, rolling back the sleeves of his button-down shirt to the forearms and geeking out over the equipment.

Almost none of the words he used to describe what he'd bought made any sense, but the smile he wore when he talked drove it all from her consciousness anyway.

She stood back and let him do his thing because... *oh, my God*, was he sexy when he got his hands dirty in his realm of expertise. This was Desmond at his finest, building something from the ground up, and he nearly glowed with some kind of inner fire she couldn't explain and couldn't stop basking in.

Once he got the mysterious settings of the computer's brain the way he wanted, he showed her how it worked, settling her into the chair and leaning over her shoulder. Something wholly masculine wafted from him as he pointed at the something-or-other on the screen, explaining that he'd done some kind of magic mojo to hook her computer into the private network housed in his workshop.

"It'll be fast," he promised. His tone indicated this was a desirable state, so she nodded. "And I have access to all of the top academic institutions and think tanks in the world. There is literally not one scrap of information discovered in the history of mankind that is not available to you via this portal."

Not one scrap? She bit her lip before asking if his computer could explain why she wanted him to kiss her so badly that her teeth ached. It was unfathomable to her how this small act of kindness and understanding had put so much of a deeper awareness of him under her skin. But it had. And what had been there before was bad enough.

This was different. Encompassing. Inevitable in some ways.

"I installed an instant messaging client, too," he continued, tapping a little blue icon on the screen. "I'll keep mine open and if you need anything while I'm working, you can let me know."

"Isn't that the equivalent of a text message?" She couldn't help but ask because... Come on. What was she going to need to say to him that she couldn't get up and walk the two flights of stairs to his workshop? Besides, she couldn't imagine bothering him with something he viewed as an uncomfortable social contract.

Unperturbed, he shrugged. "Probably. I've never used instant messaging. But schoolwork can be lonely and isolating, especially at this level. I didn't want you to feel cut off."

That turned her heart over in a completely different way because he could only know that from personal experience. And his solution to prevent her from feeling that way? Grant her special backstage access to the genius himself. It was touching, sending little fingers of warmth into her soul.

Because she couldn't stop herself, she reached out and covered his forearm with her palm. "Thank you for this."

He glanced down at her hand and then at her, seemingly just now noticing their close proximity, which only dialed up the awareness about a billion degrees. Prickles walked across her cheeks, her neck. Across her cleavage as he stared at her. They were so close she could see dark flecks in his irises.

"You're welcome."

What did it say that she'd started loving that gruff note in his voice? That she was insane, clearly. She snatched her hand back, chastising herself for falling prey to the intimacy he'd unwittingly created. It instantly disintegrated the moment she stopped touching him. He backed away quickly, heading for the door of her bedroom.

He turned before exiting, running a hand across his beard, which was holy-cow sexy all at once. "Let me know if you're missing anything."

Like her marbles? "I can't imagine what I'd need that you haven't already thought of."

Once Desmond had taken himself and his disturbing presence out of her room, she began the long, arduous process of downloading software, updating her preferences and finally logging on to the university website to figure out how online classes worked.

As the first syllabus spilled onto her screen, she had a total moment of bliss. She didn't love the pressure of academics by any stretch, but she did like a feeling of purpose and accomplishment. This was step one toward her medical degree and she longed to immerse herself in the wonders of the human body. Biology had been her favorite subject since ninth grade when she'd dissected a frog and realized the working parts were similar to other animals but not identical. How amazing was that? She'd yearned to learn more, and had in her undergraduate classes.

Now came the really good stuff.

Thanks to the husband she'd never expected to meet let alone like, she was finally on her way.

At some point Desmond returned with Conner for his next round of feeding. Des apologized for interrupting her, but she waved it off and settled into her recliner, glad for the excuse to get up from her hunched position at the desk. Once the baby was full and happy, she started to hand him back to his father when she realized there was something she could do for Desmond to thank him for his thoughtfulness.

"You know what?" McKenna pulled a fast one, shifting the baby's trajectory, and resettled Conner in her lap. "Let me play nanny for the afternoon."

Desmond quirked a brow. "That's my job."

"I know, but even you can benefit from a break occasionally. Go build something."

His smile was far too brief. "You have class work. Conner is my responsibility."

How many men would complain about being relieved of baby duty for the afternoon? Just one in her experience. "Don't be difficult. Let me do something nice for you."

"All right." He didn't sound like it was all right. He sounded like he didn't quite know what had hit him. "If you're sure."

She hefted Conner higher against her chest, supporting his downy head with her palm. "Off you go."

Actually she looked forward to spending time with Conner. She'd tried to limit her exposure to him as much as possible and, thus far, Desmond had been pretty on board with that. But diving into medical school had brought home the fact that she would not live in this house forever with easy access to her baby. Eventually she'd have to leave and as much as she'd been telling herself she couldn't wait and moaning about how Desmond's deal was too Machiavellian for words, she'd secretly started dreading the future.

"Two hours," Desmond finally agreed with a nod. "But only because you called me difficult."

So that was a sensitive subject apparently, judging by his indignant tone. She stuck her tongue out to lighten the mood. "Is that the magic button? I'll keep that in my back pocket then."

His mouth curved and he rubbed Conner's head in farewell. Desmond faded from the room but his presence lingered, made all the more strong by virtue of the new desk standing in the corner.

She'd probably never sit at it without reliving him leaning over her with the brush of his arm against hers.

"Just you and me, sport," she murmured to Conner, who picked that moment to wail in her ear. "Oh, none of that, now. Your daddy will come running, wondering what I'm doing to torture you."

McKenna rose from the chair and paced with Conner on her shoulder. Sometimes he needed extra burping after feeding. But a few rounds of gently massaging his tummy didn't get her anywhere. Diaper change, then.

She hurried to the nursery, which was down the hall between her bedroom and Desmond's. He'd decorated the room with rocket ships and stars, with a complete solar system tethered to the ceiling with thin fishing line. It was an odd choice for a baby but she'd never questioned it because it was easy to envision the man responsible for the décor lovingly placing each item exactly where he wanted it. The theme made sense to Desmond and she appreciated that he'd taken such care with the room his son would live in.

McKenna changed Conner's diaper in no time and that did the trick. No more wailing. Smiling at her little bundle of joy, she found his favorite stuffed animal—an elephant Desmond called Peter, for God knew what reason—and played peekaboo with it while Conner kicked happily from his bouncy seat.

What an amazing little person. He was gorgeous, with dark fuzzy hair and chubby cheeks. Her allotted two hours flew by and, before she'd blinked, Desmond peeked into the room with no-nonsense purpose on his face.

"I'm done building something," he informed her, his

voice smoothed out now that he was back in control. "You can do your own thing now."

"Like biochemistry?" She frowned. That had sounded so exciting earlier, before she'd had a couple of peaceful hours with her son.

"Yes, exactly like that." Desmond swooped in and effectively kicked her out with a nonchalant wave.

With far more regret than she'd like, she left father and baby to go back to her room, but she couldn't concentrate on anything. The first lesson of her biochemistry class blurred, turning into a giant mess on the screen. Looked like a swim was in order.

But as she splashed through the water, even the normally hypnotic activity didn't help. She kept craning her neck, looking for Desmond, though he'd only sought her out in the pool room twice in the six weeks she'd been living there.

Something was wrong with her. The melancholy she'd slipped into had all the hallmarks of mild depression, but she'd never been one to mope around. Of course, she'd been busy for years. This was the first real break she'd had from life since forever. Maybe that was part of her problem; she wasn't busy enough.

What more of a distraction did she need than new graduate-level courses? Desmond had provided her with the best prescription possible for her ennui and she wasn't even taking advantage of it. Maybe she should check out the other class Desmond had registered her for.

She dried off and got dressed, then resettled at her computer to access the second class. Embryology. Huh. She had a better than average understanding of that subject. The syllabus pretty much outlined the forty weeks she'd just experienced in real life: the stages from human conception through birth, with an emphasis on cellular development as the fetus grew.

Except, in her case, it wasn't a generic fetus, as she'd told herself for the entire length of her pregnancy. Neither had it turned out to be *just* an experiment to help her understand what her pregnant patients would be going through.

She'd carried Desmond's baby. Conner. He was a sweet, darling little angel who rarely cried and made her smile whenever she gazed at his face. Conner was her son, too.

A tear splashed down on the keyboard and then another. Finally she had to admit she'd thoroughly messed up in her quest to stay removed from the maternal instincts that surged to the surface on a continual basis.

Instead of a long goodbye, she'd started loving her son.

What was she going to do?

Go back to biochemistry. What else? Maybe she was just tired and could handle the embryonic course better tomorrow, when she hadn't just spent two hours in the company of the baby.

The first lesson scrolled onto the screen again. The concepts should have been easy, a review of the things she'd learned in undergraduate chemistry classes. But she couldn't get her brain to wrap around what she was reading.

A little message popped up to inform her that Desmond H. Pierce was online.

The smile his name pulled out of her went a long way toward drying up the waterworks. How freaking adorable was that man? He had one contact in his chat program—his wife—yet he found it necessary to spell out his full name?

She couldn't help herself. She clicked on the little blue icon and opened a chat window.

McKenna: *Desmond H. Pierce? Were you worried I'd confuse you with all the other Desmonds in my contact list?* Send.

She gave it fifty-fifty odds that he'd actually respond. He might even ignore her since she was essentially being a smart aleck. But the baby was obviously taking his afternoon nap. Maybe she'd get lucky.

Wonder of wonders. A message appeared under the blank window: *Desmond H. Pierce is typing.*

Desmond H. Pierce: *It asked for my name. That's what I entered.*

She actually laughed out loud at that.

McKenna: *You're so literal.*

Desmond: *Yes.*

McKenna: *Did you change your name in your settings? Just because I said something about it?*

Desmond: *Maybe.*

For some reason that pinged around her heart. She didn't take his sensitivity into account nearly often enough when she was bulldozing through aspects of his personality she actually found really great.

McKenna: *I like that you're so literal. I never have to question what you mean when you say something.*

Desmond: *You'll be very lonely in that group of one.*

McKenna: *I didn't join so I could hang out with throngs of Desmond H. Pierce admirers. I'm your wife, not a groupie.*

The chat window stayed maddeningly blank for the longest time. So long, that she started to wonder if she should apologize for something or clarify that she'd been messing around. One bad thing about virtual communication—Desmond couldn't see her face or hear her tone, so he didn't know she was kidding.

Finally the status bar told her Desmond was typing.

Desmond: *And as my wife, you're in the position to know that I have very few admirers.*

McKenna: *Because you spend all your time building fake people instead of communicating with real ones?*

Desmond: *Because the list of those who like literal people is very short.*

McKenna: *You say stuff like that all the time. I like you. You act as if there's something wrong with me because I don't see you as difficult.*

Desmond: *You don't?*

She shook her head and typed: *Duh.*

This time the pause was longer and she waited with baited breath to see what he might come back with.

Desmond: *Then I would expect it to be easier to get you on a second date.*

Her breath gasped out in a half laugh, half exhale of shock. *That* was why he thought she'd been so adamantly resistant to his perfectly chiseled mouth?

Actually she couldn't remember why resistance had been so set in her mind as a necessity. Because she didn't like the idea of getting involved with a self-confessed control addict? Yeah, Desmond liked to keep a tight fist on his son's life and held the cards of her future, as well. But he was also kind. Full of love for his son. Beyond intelligent. And a little dorky. For some reason, she liked that about him the best.

McKenna: *I would have expected you to try harder then.*

Desmond: *Is that the magic button?*

Her eyelids fluttered closed as she laughed again. What was she supposed to do with him?

McKenna: *I have lots of magic buttons.*

Probably she shouldn't be flirting with him. But it was fun. And she definitely didn't hate the long twinge that curled through her midsection as she pictured Desmond going on an exploratory mission to see how each button worked. And how many times he could press them to get her to come.

Desmond: *Aren't you supposed to be doing school-work?*

She'd flustered him. What did it mean that she could understand him so easily despite the two floors that separated them?

McKenna: *Biochemistry is hard. It's been over a year since I was in school.*

The chat window went completely still. She waited for some kind of pep talk or maybe a condemnation for her ungratefulness. After all, he'd been the one to register her. Was he mad that she'd complained?

The atmosphere shifted and she whirled to see Desmond standing in her open doorway. Her throat went tight as she took in the look on his face. Hungry. Gorgeous. Watchful. Not safe behind a virtual chat window but here, in the flesh. In her bedroom.

"Um…hi," she blurted out as her pulse triple-timed. "I wasn't expecting you."

"Let me help with your homework."

Oh, God. That was the sweetest thing. Almost better than what she'd assumed he'd come for. "You don't have to."

"I want to." He sauntered over to the desk, his long, lean body fluid and mouthwatering as he perched on the edge, his attention on her. Not the laptop. "Show me what you're having trouble with."

Somehow she didn't think it would be prudent to point out the real trouble was with her lungs and the whole breathing thing when he got this close. She shouldn't let him affect her this way. "The first lesson covers the kinetics of catalyzed versus uncatalyzed reactions."

He didn't as much as blink. "You're studying analytic chemistry in a biochemistry class?"

His knee brushed her hand. She should move it. But it was resting so comfortably on the arm of the chair and the zing of his touch had gone clear to her shoulder. Moving suddenly seemed impossible.

"Apparently." But given that he'd clued in on the distinction immediately, odds were good he knew both pretty well. Her genius husband was a resource she hadn't fully appreciated when embarking on a medical degree. "The reaction formulas the professor covers are a little different than how I learned it in undergrad."

He shifted to view the screen, his thigh snugging up next to her arm. Fireworks exploded in her core as his presence overwhelmed her system.

"Wow. That is a really roundabout way to demonstrate the transition. I have some diagrams that are far more useful than this garbage."

Leaning closer, he tapped on her keyboard, apparently oblivious to the fact that her shoulder was buried in his chest. She sucked in a breath and tried to ignore the way her muscles tensed, ready to reach out and touch him at a moment's notice. Because if she started, she feared she might not stop.

"See?" He pointed at the two-color graph on the screen that had materialized from his mystical gateway to the depths of human knowledge. "Quantify the energy transfer using this and tell me what you get."

No question in that statement because he didn't even stop to consider she might not be smart enough to follow him. He just believed she was. That wrung a whole hell of lot of something out of her heart that should not be there.

He glanced at her, his expression expectant. So she indulged them both and studied his graph. The answer popped into her head instantly.

"Gibbs free energy. 20 percent." How she squeezed that out of her mouth when her tongue had gone numb, she'd never know.

Nodding, he grinned. "Told you my stuff is better than what the professor is trying to make you use. Don't hesitate to borrow my database anytime. Or me."

That had all sorts of loaded connotations she really couldn't help but consider. Her skin flushed hot as she contemplated him and his eyes darkened as he seemed to finally pick up on the less than studious energy swirling between them.

The air fairly crackled with it as they stared at each other. How was it possible that Desmond had become that much sexier just by showing off his intelligence?

But it was an inescapable fact. Her husband's brain turned her on.

She wanted Desmond H. Pierce more than she wanted to breathe and she'd spent far too much energy denying them both something that might be spectacular, solely because she didn't want to give him any more control than he already had.

There was one surefire way to deal with that—make her own choices. If she didn't like where things were going, they signed divorce papers and went on. Easy out.

"Chemistry wasn't really part of the deal," she murmured.

His body swiveled until he was facing her instead of the computer. "I don't mind helping with your homework."

That wasn't the chemistry she was concerned about at the moment. She wanted Desmond's hands on her body and his mouth following shortly behind, but she'd put up so many roadblocks it was no wonder he was practicing what she'd preached, namely that getting involved was a bad idea.

There were probably a host of things she should carefully consider before throwing caution to the wind. But right this minute, she didn't care. There was nothing separating them but her own unfounded fears.

Seven

Biochemistry. That was the chemistry Des should be focusing on, but he'd frankly lost all interest in McKenna's class work in favor of drowning in her expressive gaze. Her eyes held a whole world inside them and he couldn't stop drinking it in.

The draw between him and his wife was a whole other kind of chemistry, the kind he'd like to learn about because he had the distinct feeling there'd be a lot to absorb.

"My homework will be there later," McKenna informed him throatily. The slight rasp in her voice hooked him instantly. It meant she was as affected by his nearness as he was hers.

The desk had been an altruistic gift, solely designed to get her started on her degree. He hadn't considered that it would become a method of seduction. But the object of his affection sat within arm's length in the chair he'd selected for her. His leg had been in firm contact with her hand for the better part of five minutes but she hadn't rolled away.

"When is your first lesson due?" he asked. The last thing he wanted to do was distract her when she'd just started what looked to be a difficult class given how backward the instructor planned to teach something as straightforward as chemical reactions.

"I don't know." She didn't take her gaze from his and he couldn't look away, not when she had so many interesting nonverbal things she was saying. "But it's not right this minute. We have plenty of time to worry about that later."

College classes had definitely shifted his advantage and he was nothing if not prepared to press it.

Awareness saturated the atmosphere. So maybe she was looking for a distraction. One that had a much more explosive reaction than those detailed on her screen.

"McKenna," he murmured, and her face tipped up to the perfect angle for him to take her mouth with his, which he planned to do as soon as he was clear on whether he'd been reading her signals correctly.

Once he kissed her, he didn't plan to stop. Therefore, it would be prudent to make sure that's what she wanted.

"Desmond," she murmured back.

The way she caressed his name with her raspy voice settled low in his gut, flaring out with sensual heat that would take little to stoke higher. The virtual chat had gotten him good and primed already, especially with all the talk of magic buttons.

He should have installed a chat tool weeks ago. Who knew that would be the mechanism to get his wife to flirt with him?

But virtual chatting only went so far. Being in her presence heightened the reactions her sexy talk had started and he craved the experience of connecting with her in the flesh. There was so much to discover between them, nuances of emotion and heights of pleasure to catalog. He couldn't wait to start exploring.

"I'm going to kiss you," he informed her. "If that's not what you want, you should tell me to leave. Immediately."

Her dark eyes speared him to the core, blazing with unmistakable heat. "My mouth is one of my buttons."

As invitations went, that couldn't be much clearer. But they'd been at this spot before and she'd backed off. Twice. He wasn't going to make that mistake again. "And I definitely plan to push it. Along with several others. If that's not okay, I need to know that now."

"I want you to kiss me, Desmond."

Her exasperation came through loud and clear but he'd been exasperated for nearly a week. She could deal with it until he had the answers he needed.

"What about the complications?" he asked.

She stood so fast that the chair shot backward and tipped over, but he could hardly focus on anything other than the beautiful woman who'd stepped into the gap of his thighs. He widened his legs to give her plenty of room, aching to slip his hands around her waist and yank her closer to his center. Her heat was exactly what his throbbing erection needed.

"The only complication I'm dealing with right now is the one between your ears," she said with a half laugh as her hands slid over his shoulders. "I'm starting to see how you could be described as difficult."

Apparently impatient with waiting, she wound her fist in his shirt and pulled. He let her because… *Hell, yes*, this was the chemistry he'd come for. If she wanted to move things forward at her own pace, he wasn't going to argue.

And then their mouths aligned, both rough and tender at the same time. It was such a rush of sensation that his entire body jolted. The kiss deepened without any effort on his part as she inhaled him, drawing him into her spirit and essence with nothing more than the conduit of her mouth.

She was molten and fluid, eager. Best of all, she'd granted him permission to drop down the rabbit hole with her.

Now he could touch. With the threat of losing this moment eliminated, he smoothed his palms down her back, reveling in the firmness of her body against his fingertips. *His wife.* The mother of his child. She felt unbelievable and that was saying something considering how often he'd fantasized about having her this close, this available for his investigation.

And the kiss deepened even further, destroying him from the inside out as she nestled against the planes of his torso, thigh to thigh.

Her hot tongue slid forward, seeking and… Oh, yes, he craved more of that, already anticipating the way she filled him with her taste. He took each thrust, felt it in his bones, his blood, his groin. She crawled inside him easily and he didn't try to stop the flood of McKenna. She was right where he wanted her.

He let her have her fun for four seconds. *My turn.*

Nearly drunk on her, he wrested control of the kiss away from her in one fell swoop, spinning to capture her against the desk. His thigh spread hers and she gasped, but opened to him beautifully, accepting his hard length at her center with surprising willingness. Stars exploded across his vision as he absorbed her heat through his clothes.

She was so ready for him. Probably slick with it and swollen. He could feel her desire under his skin, where the empathy was always strongest, and it built his own need to a fevered pitch.

More. Now. He gripped her jaw and slanted it, plunging into her mouth with a ferocity he had no idea he possessed. But she met him halfway, seemingly as impatient for it as he was. Desperate little moans vibrated from her throat and it thrilled him to incite such sounds of abandon from her.

She wanted him. Wanted the connection he'd felt from the first. The sense of isolation and loneliness he'd carried for most of his life vanished in a snap as he opened his soul to what she was offering him.

Warm hands branded his back as she explored under his shirt. He returned the favor, yanking the fabric of her T-shirt from her pants and letting his fingers do the talking. Beautiful. Velvety. He couldn't get enough of her skin. Too many clothes in the way.

"Desmond," she breathed against his mouth.

He scarcely had enough of his senses left to recognize his own name. "Hmm." Her throat had the tenderest little area that his lips fit into perfectly and he got busy acquainting himself with it as he slipped the T-shirt off her shoulder to give him better access.

"I hate to mention it, but I'm, um…not on any kind of birth control. I wasn't expecting this."

That heavy dose of reality put a pall over the wonders of her skin against his tongue. He lifted his head, his mind clicking through all the possible scenarios as the critical pieces of information fell into their buckets. She didn't want to get pregnant again. Of course she didn't. And, idiot that he was, he hadn't been expecting her to remove all the obstacles between them so quickly either. Why hadn't he had an entire truckload of condoms delivered? Some genius he was.

But surely he was smart enough to salvage the situation.

"No problem," he murmured and slid a hand under her shirt to toy with her bra strap. "We're just getting started. There's a lot of you I haven't seen yet and a lot of ways I can make love to you that don't require birth control."

Her eyes darkened. "I'm thoroughly intrigued by that statement."

"Let me demonstrate."

He lifted the hem of her shirt and whipped it off. The catch on her bra came apart in his fingers with a small snick and her lush, full breasts spilled out before he could fully peel the fabric from them.

Groaning as he tossed her clothes to the floor, he packed both palms with her engorged flesh. Erect nipples chafed his hands and the heat of her zinged through his erection. There was no way he could have been more turned on in that moment.

"I need to see the rest of you," he said hoarsely, and she nodded, pulling off her pants and underwear in one motion.

Naked, she perched on the desk without an ounce of embarrassment. Slowly he settled into her desk chair and caressed her thighs, trailing down to her knees. Then pushed, opening her until she was spread wide. She didn't protest, just shoved the computer aside so she could lean back on her elbows, letting him look his fill. It was the most humbling experience of his life, except for the first moment he'd held his son. This woman had given him both.

"McKenna," he murmured and it fell from his lips like a prayer. "I can't believe how gorgeous you are."

Laying his lips on her thigh, he worked his way toward

her center. She squirmed restlessly, gasping as he abraded her tender flesh with his beard, which he'd thankfully trimmed not too long ago. It was about to come in very handy as he pleasured his wife.

The first lick in her slick center pulled a cry from her that thickened his erection past the point of all reason. *How* was she so sexy, so disturbing, in all the best ways? He'd barely started and her taste exploded against his lips as she rolled her hips, shimmying closer to his mouth.

Obviously she wanted him to go deeper. That worked for him. He gave it to her, grasping her hips to hold her still as she couldn't seem to manage that on her own. Excellent. He loved that she got so into it, crying and panting with little feminine noises as he licked her harder.

He twisted two fingers into her slick channel, gently because he was nothing if not overly sensitive to the fact that she'd recently given birth to the miracle that lay sleeping down the hall.

She bucked, her muscles clamping down beautifully on his fingers in a release that tensed her whole body. Throbbing with his own desire, he nibbled at her core until she came again, crying his name and rocking against his tongue.

The most amazing feeling washed over him and it was so engulfing, so beautiful. He couldn't sort whether he'd sensed it from her or it had bloomed from his depths. Didn't matter. They were so entwined, so connected, they'd probably generated it together. Simultaneously. It was nearly spiritual. He needed more.

"Again," he murmured and started all over.

She shook her head and tried to move out of reach, but he clamped down on her hips.

"I want to return the favor," she insisted weakly, levering higher on her elbows to capture his gaze and, without looking away or letting her do so either, he took a long, slow lick at that precise moment.

She shuddered, banked embers in her depths flaring to life in a raging fire that stoked his own.

"That can wait," he informed her. "This can't. I've dreamed about having you at my mercy, exactly in this position. You took biology. You know the tongue is the strongest muscle in the body. I can do this all night."

Her eyelids fluttered closed as he spread her again with his thumbs and proved his point by giving her the flat of his tongue. Her swollen folds welled again as she orgasmed a third time in mere seconds.

"Stop, it's too much," she gasped and then cursed as he ignored her, wholly unsatisfied with how little he'd done for her. How could a few orgasms possibly compare with what he owed her? She'd sacrificed a year of her life in pursuit of his plan for a family and delayed medical school to nourish his son.

"It's not enough," he corrected, his lips still buried inside her. "I'm only just beginning to learn which buttons to push. I need a lot more research between your thighs before I can possibly stop. For example, what does this button do?"

He rubbed his beard right in the center of the bundle of sensitized nerves. She cried out as she came again, her back lifting off the desk in an arch that thrust her breasts skyward. It was such an erotic pose that he nearly lost the iron grip he had on his own release. The need to fill her, to finally empty himself inside her, overwhelmed him and he almost couldn't stand it.

"Please, Desmond," she nearly sobbed. "I want…need. Something. More. You."

Maybe they'd both had enough. It was all he could do

to keep from stripping down and giving her what she'd asked for. No condom, just flesh on flesh for an eternity.

Reluctantly he pulled back and kissed her inner thigh. This interlude had merely been the precursor and he wasn't opposed to giving her time to recover. "We'll have it your way. More of that later tonight."

"I don't think I'll be recovered by then," she muttered and then shot him a sly smile. "And don't think I've forgotten how merciless you are. I will definitely be returning that part of the favor, as well."

We'll see about that. He had several hours to get condoms into this house and maybe a few other surprises that would guarantee she wouldn't back off again.

That was the most important thing. The less time he gave her to second-guess what was happening here, the better. He wasn't nearly finished exploring how deep this unbelievable coupling between them went.

Funny how he'd once been so determined to deconstruct their attraction solely with the intent of making it stop. Now that he'd started, he never wanted it to end.

Desmond finally left her alone after promising he had something special in mind for later that night. McKenna ate dinner in the kitchen with Mrs. Elliot and a couple of the groundskeepers, which was fairly typical, but she couldn't seem to swallow.

Anticipation kept her whole body keyed up. Throwing caution to the wind had allowed for an amazing experience at the hands—and mouth—of her husband. Frankly she couldn't imagine what else he might come up with that could top earlier. But she was totally game to find out.

After dinner, McKenna fed the baby and put him down for the night. If true to form, Conner would sleep until midnight. Four hours away.

As she hurried to her room to get dressed for her date with Desmond, she didn't pretend to have anything on her mind other than what might be considered "special." The things he'd done to her body… She hadn't realized she could come that hard or that many times in a row. Or that she'd married a man who wasn't done after giving her one orgasm. He should teach a class—in her experience, that wasn't the typical philosophy of the male gender as a whole. So far, she was a huge fan of Desmond's brand of lovemaking.

And if all the stars aligned, she'd get to learn a lot more about his philosophies. She shuddered as her body got in on the anticipation in its own way, soaking the tiny scrap of silk underwear she'd slipped on. So much for wearing sexy lingerie for her husband. Maybe he'd like it if she went commando.

Why was she so *nervous*? It wasn't like she'd never had sex before. And, for all intents and purposes, she'd *already* had sex with Desmond. The big difference, of course, being that this time he'd be participating.

The knock on her door nearly separated her skin from her bones. She smoothed the skirt of the dress she'd painstakingly picked, though it probably didn't matter. It would likely be on the floor shortly.

She opened the door and her breath caught as Desmond's gaze devoured her whole.

"Come with me," he said simply and held out his hand.

Her palm in his, she let him lead her down the hall to his bedroom. All righty then. No preamble apparently. This wasn't a date in the traditional sense, with wine and flowers. They were just going to hop into bed? Of course, given her abandon earlier, she couldn't exactly claim a sense of modesty or that she needed romance to get her motor going. Desmond pretty much just had to look at her and her panties melted.

But then he ushered her through the double doors, clicking them closed behind him as the darkness of the room surrounded her. Her pulse leaped, hammering in her throat as her pupils fought to adjust to the black.

"I hope you meant what you said about liking thunderstorms." His voice slid across her skin like silk a moment before a rumble sounded from the far wall.

A bolt of lightning forked across the ceiling in a brief flash of light. Awestruck, she watched as another one streaked across the wall. "You made me a thunderstorm?"

"I did." Another rumble of thunder interrupted him, louder this time, as if the storm was growing closer. "Surprise."

"It's brilliant." Lightning lit up the room for another brief second, revealing the four-poster. Somehow, the faux storm swirled around it, beckoning her straight into the center.

But Desmond didn't give her a chance to take one step. Sweeping her up into his arms, he carried her to the bed, laying her out on the comforter. "It took some doing. I think it turned out well."

The patter of rain echoed behind her head, coming faster now as more thunder crashed through the bedframe, shaking it with shocking realism. "I don't think you could have made it more real."

"Let's just see about that, shall we?" Lightning illuminated half his face, revealing a wicked smile that put a tingle in her breasts.

Faint music danced between the crashes of thunder, something electronic and fast with no lyrics that kept time with the storm perfectly, as if one fed the other. The divine maestro himself rolled onto the mattress, sweeping her into his arms and into the maelstrom with a hot, hungry kiss.

Instantly her body electrified. With her eyes closed, she could scarcely credit how real the storm seemed. Desmond's tongue circled hers, demanding and insistent. White-hot desire split her core, flooding her with the thick, achy need that only he could satisfy.

In the space of one peal of thunder, he pulled off her dress and crouched over her. The next time the room lit up, his gaze traveled over her, hot and heavy.

"I, um, thought it was going to be my turn to be merciless," she squeaked as he bent to mouth her throat. Her head tipped back involuntarily to give him better access. When his fingers slipped under the cups of the bra to lightly play with her nipples, her back bowed off the bed, grinding her pelvis into his.

Every erogenous zone on her body was far more sensitive than she was used to but her breasts were the worst. Best. His touch penetrated her to the marrow, swept a volcanic wave through her blood until she was writhing under the press of his hips, silently begging him for what she'd only gotten a taste of earlier.

"Please," she rasped. "I want your mouth on me again."

His lips were nearly poetic, strong, full, talented. And she wanted his French kiss between her legs immediately. She'd get busy pleasuring him very, very soon, but she couldn't help how much the earlier session on the desk had prepped her for a repeat.

"Absolutely in the plan," he murmured. "We have hours and I intend to use every last second to worship your body."

His fingers tangled in her bra straps, pulling them down off her shoulders until both breasts burst free of their confines. The first scratch of his beard against a nipple raced down her spine, unleashing a shiver. But he didn't draw the aching tip into his mouth like she'd expected, somehow cluing in that she'd had enough stimulation in that area lately.

Instead he laved at the underside, finding new places to nibble that she'd have never called sensitive, but he lit her up with nothing more than carefully placed teeth.

Gasping, she twisted against the onslaught, nearly weeping to get more of him against her flesh. He complied, inching his way down her stomach with his fiery mouth, leaving trails of sensation as he went until he hit the juncture of her thighs, where she ached for him most.

"You're not wearing any panties," he announced, a thread of pure lust lacing his voice. "It's almost as if you're asking for me to spend a lot of time down here."

Breathless, she choked out a laugh. "You read my mind."

By way of answer, his slightly rough and wholly talented hands slid up her thighs and pressed, opening her wide until her knees hit the comforter on either side. His hands—she couldn't get enough of them on her. They spoke a language all their own as his thumbs explored her center, rubbing, dipping, whirling her into an oblivion of sensation heightened by simultaneous booms of thunder and the drumming of rain.

The heat and pressure of his mouth at her core as he finally added his lips and tongue tensed her whole body, and the gush of wetness was almost embarrassing, except he groaned, lapping it up.

"So gorgeous. So responsive. I love how I can do this to you," he said and swirled his tongue with exactly the right motion to send a shower of heat through her as she slid to the edge and over, rippling through the first of what would likely be many spectacular climaxes.

"Again," she commanded, instantly addicted to his talents, delirious with the pleasure of his hands. "But this time with you."

She'd waited long enough. She wanted to see him, to touch. To bring him to climax and hear him cry out because the release was too big to keep inside. Rolling away from him before he could clamp down on her thighs again, because she knew his tricks now, she knelt on the bed and pushed at his shoulders, insisting he sit up from his position on all fours.

It clearly amused him to do as she directed since he did it. Otherwise she'd probably never have moved him. Honestly, it was a crapshoot on whether she'd have rolled back under his mouth if he hadn't. Her core still quivered from the climax and she well knew the second one would be even better. Her body craved it, demanded it, sought it with little circles of her hips even as she fingered her way down his shirt in the dark, unbuttoning as she went.

He was lucky she didn't tear the thing from his body, shedding buttons like flower petals ripped from their stems. Finally she drew off the shirt and couldn't resist her first taste of Desmond's body.

Without hesitation, she bent her head and kissed his shoulder, then dragged her tongue across his clavicle. His hands gripped her waist, holding her in place as he sucked in a breath. Bolder now, she nipped at his throat, nibbled her way up the column to his ear and laved at his lobe, eliciting a groan deep in his chest that thrilled her.

This was her turn and she suddenly wanted to lavish him with as much care as he'd showed her. She pushed him back onto the mattress and rid him of his pants and underwear. She wished she could have done a slow reveal but she wanted to touch.

Warm flesh pulsed under her palms as she covered

him and, in that moment, the thunder and lightning crashed simultaneously, lighting up the bed well enough for her to see the gorgeous length. Tongue to the tip, she licked, her eyes on him, his eyes on her.

Darkness fell again but the half-lidded expression of pure pleasure on his face had burned into her mind. She sucked the whole of him into her mouth, rolling her tongue around his shaft until he groaned out her name, hips pistoning under her palms.

"Enough," he growled and she almost ignored him as he'd done to her earlier, but he easily lifted her off him and set her back against the pillow, thumb sliding across her face in an apologetic caress. "You can have many orgasms but my physiology isn't as evolved and your mouth is amazing."

Fair enough. A rustle indicated he'd likely donned a condom and delicious anticipation filled her. This was it. The consummation of all of this foreplay.

Thunder cracked again and again, heightening the low throb in her core. He didn't make her wait. Before she could blink, he'd gathered her up and laid her down, covering her with his hot, firm body. But instead of gearing up to plunge in, he captured her lips in a long, tender kiss.

Slowly his tongue explored hers. The rush swept outward, languorously stealing over her skin as he made love to her mouth. This kiss wasn't about the mechanics of sex, which he'd proved again and again he had down pat. It was the basest form of communication and she absorbed all of what he was saying, grasping it eagerly with every fiber of her body.

"I want you," he said over and over, and it was a delicious kick to be the object of his desire. His hand drifted down her arm, caressing, lingering, then eventually working south to her waist, her thigh. The gorgeous,

heavy press of his body on hers grew more insistent. He shifted, hips rolling suggestively against hers. The kiss deepened, grew urgent, and she answered with her own suggestive shimmy and slid her thigh along his, opening herself up into a wide cradle.

"McKenna."

He murmured her name so reverently it curled through her senses. Her head tipped back against the pillow as she felt him slide into place at her core. Then he pushed and his thick length filled her, and it was so right, she gasped. Urgency overtook them both and they came together in perfect tempo with the music and the rain and the fevered ecstasy he was building in every pore of her body.

Soaring, she gave up all thought, reason, let him fill her to the brim with the pretty phrases he drizzled down on her as they wound each other higher and higher. At the crescendo of the next round of thunder, his gifted fingers danced across the button at her center, firm, hot, and it shattered her. Boneless, she came, rippling around his length in a powerful release that eclipsed anything she'd ever known. Wave after wave of something divine swamped her, spiraling her into a near out-of-body experience.

But she didn't want to be out of her body, not when Desmond was still powering through the finale of his own release. Hands on his back, she urged him on, whispering encouragement until he tensed against her thighs with a hoarse cry.

It was so beautiful, tears slid down her face.

Collapsing to the mattress, he rolled her into his arms, holding her tight against his body, wordless. No matter. The nonverbal spoke loudly enough in the darkness.

Wow.

After a long, delicious eternity of nothing but naked

skin against hers, he nuzzled her ear. "Tell me that was fantastic for you."

She nodded far less enthusiastically than she'd have liked but her muscles were still recovering. "Fantastic is an understatement."

"I…felt it," he murmured, sounding hesitant for the first time since he'd swept her into the room. "Your pleasure, I mean. It was like a second presence and it was unbelievably amazing. It's hard to explain and now I'm sure you think I'm as weird as everyone else does."

He trailed off with a half laugh but she sat up, scowling, even though he couldn't see her until lightning forked across the ceiling on the next wave.

"Stop it. I do not think you're weird." *Different*, sure. But in a good way. "You're brilliant and kind and you made me a thunderstorm. If that's weird, then weird should be considered the new sexy."

"You think I'm sexy?"

Her eye roll was so loud, it was a wonder he hadn't heard it. "Duh. I can't even count all of my orgasms today."

"Six. So far."

Dear God. "No. Not *so far*. Absolutely no more. For me anyway. It's your turn."

He'd stopped her before she could finish the job she'd started earlier and if any more orgasms happened tonight, they'd be all his.

"I'm afraid that's not going to work for me." His hand found hers, clasped it. Twined their fingers together. "I like it when you come and I like having my mouth on you when it happens. It's so much better than anything I've ever imagined."

He yanked on their clasped hands, pulling her off balance. She fell to the mattress and he covered her immediately. She squirmed and only succeeded in grinding against his semi-erection.

"That was dirty," she snapped as he trapped her against the pillow, arms above her head.

"Not sorry. By the way, if you think you've experienced the full extent of my imagination, you'd be wrong."

She shuddered as he slid down the length of her body to nip at the juncture between her legs. There was a half second when she considered clamping her thighs together to prove a point. But then her knees fell open almost without any help on her part as he pushed on them. Who the hell was she kidding? As if she had the power to deny him access to whatever he wanted to lick, touch or bite on her body.

Delirious instantly, she thrashed under his hot mouth, so many emotions bleeding through her chest. His teeth scraped across her nub and she nearly screamed as white-hot pleasure crashed against the realization that her feelings for him went far deeper than she'd guessed.

The flood of everything crested up and over as he increased the pressure exactly as he'd learned—so quickly—would splinter her into a million pieces. The wave of her release spread like molten lava, eating up all her cold, empty places and filling them with Desmond.

This was not supposed to be happening.

Furious with herself for letting things get so out of hand, she clenched against her release, cutting it short through sheer will.

"McKenna," he murmured. "Let go. Don't deny yourself because I wished to pleasure you instead of letting you have your way."

She nearly laughed and then choked on it as he did something new against her core. The sensation gripped her in steely claws, coaxing her back to the edge. And then he pushed her over with a shattering climax that put the other six to shame.

Her husband commanded her body as easily as he'd commanded her to wait for the divorce. She'd given him that power by choosing intimacy and it scared her all at once. She didn't know if she *could* deny this draw between them.

"That was so beautiful," he said and curled her against his side. "You're my wife and you deserve to be treated like a queen. Think of me as your vassal. Sleep here. I'll bring Conner to you and put him back to bed. You do nothing more strenuous than lay here until morning. Sleep if you want. Or tell me to pleasure you again."

She blinked and settled her palm on his chest, content to lay half on top of him because he felt delicious against her overused muscles. That was the problem with Desmond. He made it sound like she'd gotten it all wrong, that he was the most selfless human on the planet. She didn't have to do anything but lounge around and wait for the next time she felt like ordering her husband to make her body sing?

If there was a downside to that, she couldn't find it.

Eight

Carefully, Desmond eased back into the bed after checking on the baby for the second time. Conner had started waking up at 6:00 a.m. two nights ago, but both times Des had been able to get him to go back to sleep without nursing.

The material he'd read suggested that if he let the baby eat, he would eat. If his father talked him back into bed without giving him what he wanted, Conner learned that he didn't have to eat just because his eyes were open. So far, so good.

McKenna lay in Desmond's bed, eyes closed and face tranquil. He'd kept her awake far past when he should have but once he'd started exploring the wonders of her, he couldn't stop. She hadn't complained. And he intended to ensure that continued to be the case.

Des had turned off the storm machine before the baby's midnight feeding, which was a necessary shame. That had been inspired and McKenna had loved it. Conner wouldn't have. Last night was the first time his wife had breast-fed his son in Desmond's bed. That unprecedented event deserved respect, as did the fact that she was still in his bed.

The first of many nights if he had anything to say about it.

He had no practice at sliding between the covers without waking another person. Somehow he levered himself onto the mattress without rocking it, then got most of his body into position, a feat considering McKenna slept with abandon, flinging an arm across his pillow and curling her legs up onto his side. He didn't mind. She had gorgeous legs.

But when he pulled the covers up, they caught on something. He yanked before realizing she'd balled up a good bit in her fist.

Her dark eyes blinked open and she smirked. "Don't tell me you're an early riser. That's grounds for divorce."

He smiled because he couldn't help himself. When he looked at her, it was like seeing the sun peek through the clouds after three days of gray. "I was checking on Conner. I didn't mean to wake you up. If you weren't hogging the covers, you never would have known I'd moved."

Long, dark hair spilled over his pillow and he resisted the urge to gather it in his hands. Barely.

"Oh, I see. This is all my fault. The fact that you handcuffed me to the bed and wouldn't let me leave doesn't have anything to do with it."

His brows shot up involuntarily as he eyed her. "Even without an eidetic memory, I would have remembered if handcuffs had been involved at any point."

Had she felt like he'd forced her to sleep here last night? That was so far from his intent.

He ran through the events again, calculating, reevaluating. She'd been so into everything, eager, enthusiastic. Nearly crippling him with her desire at times as his empathy soared along with her.

There was no way he'd misread her pleasure. Or that she'd been more than willing to sleep in his bed. When he was this in tune with her, he'd know if she'd been unhappy.

"Seven orgasms," she said, holding up the requisite number of fingers in case he wasn't clear on the count. "What woman in her right mind would sleep alone after that?"

"I see. You're a slave to my attention, is that it? I've shackled you with my orgasms."

She sighed lustily. "Yeah, I guess that's true."

Something eased in his chest and he didn't hesitate to gather her up against his body so he could say good morning in a much more hands-on fashion. "In that case, we have a couple of hours until breakfast."

She groaned. "Seriously? I'm not used to this much, uh…stimulation. I haven't used some of those muscles in years."

That pleased him to no end. They'd had little to no communication about their respective love lives, but he'd envisioned that she'd been in school long enough to have avoided personal attachments. Of course, last night had been confirmation that she didn't have a boyfriend waiting in the wings.

He frowned. That was a huge assumption on his part. Women had multiple sexual partners all the time.

A growl nearly erupted from his throat but he bit it back. McKenna was his wife and after last night, he wanted to keep it that way. "Seriously. Was I not clear enough that you don't have to move? I do all the work. You have no other job than to issue instructions as you see fit. 'Harder, Des' works. 'Put your mouth on me.' These are not strenuous sentences to utter."

She laughed and flipped over to curl up in his arms spoon style. "You were clear. But the only thing I want right now is a massage."

Her shoulder nudged his chin and he didn't hesitate to put his hands on her. Cradling her firm rear with his hips, he nestled her closer and rubbed her arms with long, slow strokes. Her lengthy sigh had all the hallmarks of a woman relaxing and it settled the beastly possession that had welled up a moment ago. Mostly. He needed to get a lot more of her under his fingertips before he'd fully unwind.

McKenna. He got serious about her request and moved into a better position to take care of the one need his wife had at this moment. They'd both shed their nightclothes after the midnight feeding, which meant there was nothing in his way. He touched her at will, reveling in the soft silkiness of her skin, kneading her shoulders, curling his thumbs around the base of her skull to press along the meridians his one foray into Shiatsu had taught him would relieve her soreness.

The strongest sense of peace radiated from her flesh as he touched her and he absorbed it like a sponge. She moaned as he shifted his fingers to the top of her head, but he didn't need the additional verification that he'd also soothed her as he soothed himself.

As his fingers drifted down to caress her neck and shoulders, she arched her back, intensifying the rub of her very fine backside against the beginning of an arousal that was about to get out of hand if she didn't quit with the sensual contact. She'd asked for a massage. That's what he was giving her, as ordered.

The second time she circled her bottom to brush his

erection, fire shot through his groin. A groan rumbled from his chest. If that was an accident, he'd apologize profusely for the mistake. Later. He slid a hand down her stomach to hold her still as he ground his hips against her gorgeous, firm rear, sliding straight along the crevice. Hot. Tight.

She gasped, desire drenching her aura. And her center, as he discovered the moment he dipped his fingers into the valley between her legs. Nudging his knee between hers, he created a gap that gave him just enough access to explore.

"Desmond," she muttered breathlessly. "What happened to my massage?"

"Still going on." To prove it, he rubbed her nub with two fingers and kneaded her buttocks with the other hand, separating the twin globes enough to slide between them much more deeply than the first time.

His eyelids shuttered closed as the pressure built. He needed to be inside her, to let her take him under, to experience all of her glorious emotion in tandem with his as he built her toward release.

"That feels…i-incredible," she stuttered. "I didn't know that was one of my buttons."

"Now we both know." The heat engulfed him as he teased her backside and he couldn't hold on. Yesterday his restraint had been…well, not easy, but *easier*, solely because he hadn't yet coupled with her. Now that he had, his body had a mind of its own, desperate for her, for the sensation of being one with this woman.

Just as he was about to notch himself in the center of her slick heat for the long, slow slide to perfection, she half rolled away.

"Where are the condoms?" she asked. "You're going to need one after all."

Uh, that was a minor detail he'd conveniently forgotten. Blindly he felt around for the dresser behind him until his fingers closed over the knob and then the packets inside. Thankfully he managed to hang on to the one he grabbed and get it on before he lost his mind.

In moments, his wife's core enveloped him fully and he paused to let the scorching, flawless, rightness of her wash over him. She squirmed restlessly, not on board with slow, apparently. The decision was taken from him as his body began to crave the sweet burn of movement. As she urged him on with small hip rolls that drove him deeper inside, he rode the wave, spiraling higher and higher toward bliss.

But the real bliss lay in her reactions, every cry, all the nuance of her pleasure that heightened his own. It was everything he wanted and nothing he'd ever experienced.

Before his brain could engage, she guided his hand back to her center and he willingly started all over with the massage, but with laser focus on her erogenous zones until she rippled and squeezed through a release that shot fireworks through his gut.

Imagine if she hadn't insisted on condoms. This dazzling experience could include so much more than just an orgasm. He could impregnate her. Today. If she conceived, he could watch her grow round with his child. He'd missed that the first time and it was an injustice he ached to rectify.

His own release exploded from his depths without any warning. As he cried out through the tense burst that left him emptied, he held her close in case she had a mind to roll away. He didn't want to miss a moment of being inside her. Not one moment of making love to his wife.

She was far more than the mother of his child. She was a crucial part of the fabric of the family he'd been trying to create. How had he missed that a family of two was nice but three was so much better, especially when they were so tightly knit together already?

McKenna resettled his arm across her stomach more closely, burrowing against his chest to let him hold her as snugly as he wanted. The problem was that she'd eventually leave the bed. And his life. For all the talk about handcuffs, he had few mechanisms at his disposal to convince a woman that she should wish to stay exactly where she was.

"I need a bath," she murmured. "And maybe a nap. By *myself*."

The stress on that part came with a playful smack to his hand, which had apparently gotten too friendly with the curve of her breast. "That's the exact opposite of what I need."

"Well, I can't lie. This has been amazing. But maybe it's best if it's a one-time thing."

Something cold and sad crowded into his chest. Of course that was her thought. She'd been backing away from him since the beginning. Except now he had a stake in convincing her she didn't want to do that.

"Best for what?" he growled. "Did I dissatisfy you in some way?"

"What? No." She laughed and half rolled toward him, which pulled her from his arms. "This was just a... I don't know, a fling. An affair. I have no idea what kids call it these days. But it's not the kind of thing you keep doing, no matter how great it is."

That literally made zero sense. "Why not?"

"Because. We're getting a divorce." Exasperation laced her tone, inciting his own frustration. "This is a temporary situation until we can sort something out to get the baby weaned."

"Which we've already established may not happen for several months. Why put an arbitrary end date on something we're both happy with?" he countered far less smoothly than he'd have liked. But she was growing upset and empathy bled through him in a wholly unpleasant internal storm.

The blackness crowding his chest wasn't just his own reaction to the subject, though he had plenty of gloom vying for space. His was because he didn't know how to let her go. Hers was because she wanted him to.

"I'm just not the type to sleep with a man solely because he's generous in bed." She'd moved back to her pillow, clutching the sheet around her breasts in an ineffective cover that did nothing but heighten her sexiness. "This was maybe a blip in judgment at best. You're very difficult to say no to."

By design. He left nothing to chance, not when it was something he wanted. That meant he still had work to do if he wished to create the family he saw in his head. Everyone else in his life spent a great deal of energy trying to get away from him. McKenna was no different.

She was just the first one he wanted to stop from leaving.

The connection he craved, the one that had driven him to create a son with this woman, had flourished with McKenna in ways he'd never have imagined—and he had a great imagination. He couldn't cut it off, didn't have any desire to.

He nodded as if he agreed, his mind sifting through a hundred different scenarios that might work to change the tide of his future. If his wife wasn't the type to sleep with a man solely because he was generous in bed, then maybe she was the type to do so if he was generous out of bed.

Divorcing McKenna was not what he wanted any longer. He liked being married. To her. If she hadn't come to the realization that her future lay with him, then he would have to help her along. Provide incentives.

Orgasms were only one of many things he could offer that might convince her she'd found a permanent home in his bed and his life.

McKenna took her newfound sense of propriety and left Desmond's bed, determined not to repeat the mistake of yesterday. And last night. And again this morning. Twice.

While she'd been fumbling around for the proper terminology to describe the act of sleeping with one's husband—besides the obvious one called *marriage*—he'd been quietly campaigning to prove her completely incapable of resisting him.

As if the first time hadn't been enough of a clue. *Massage.* Leave it to Desmond to redefine that word into "explosive sexual encounter." And then follow it up with a second round that had somehow ended up with her on top, riding him with fluid, delicious motion that put the most sensually hot expression on his face. She could have watched him get lost in pleasure for an hour.

It was high time for a break from the maestro of the storm who'd lured her into sleeping with him all night long and confused her with his insistence that he was at her command instead of the other way around. She'd already been confused enough, what with her chest hurting at the thought of leaving the baby behind when the divorce was finalized.

Schoolwork beckoned. It was no easier to concentrate at her brand-new desk than it had been yesterday. Harder actually. The little blue icon in her system tray beckoned her to open it and connect with the man on the other side.

The chat tool had kindly alerted her that Desmond was online about halfway through her attempt at the second conversion exercise in her biochemistry class.

She ignored it and focused. The concepts were supposed to be a review of what she'd already mastered. So far, all she'd proved was that she could only get through this with the help of someone much smarter.

No. She wasn't too dim-witted to figure this out. She was just…preoccupied. Slowly she fought through the web of Desmond and Conner spinning through her mind and found a rhythm to the chaos. This was medical science. Her wheelhouse. A man and a baby would not—could not—distract her from getting her degree. Being a wife and mother was nothing more than a temporary glitch in her life. Nothing she'd ever wanted or seen for herself.

Her concentration improved drastically when she finally accessed Desmond's magic portal. It wasn't just a flippant label; the thing really was magic, producing results easily from her search terms. Why had she resisted this so long? He'd offered it to her and she'd pretended it didn't exist, just like she was pretending the man didn't exist. Both to her detriment.

She found some great papers online at Johns Hopkins University that walked her through the concepts in a whole different way that suddenly clicked everything together in her brain. The rest of the exercises were easy once she had the foundation straight.

Or they would have been if she'd had a chance to finish. A knock on her open door interrupted her near the end. *Desmond.* Here for the next round of nursing. Total and complete awareness of his presence invaded her very pores, skimming along her skin, raising the hair on her arms.

"Sorry to bother you," he said.

He definitely needed to find a different greeting. "I'm pretty sure I've told you it's no bother."

Conner's little baby noises finished killing her concentration where Desmond had left off. She stood from the desk to get comfortable in the rocker, already familiar and content with the routine Desmond had instituted where he took care of everything and fetched whatever she needed.

At her command. What a kick that was to have such a sensual, intelligent man wallowing at her feet.

Something far deeper than mere awareness of said man with the baby in his arms walloped her out of nowhere. He'd always drawn her eye with his energy, his classic cheekbones and dark swept-back hair. But now she knew every contour under that powder blue button-down, both visually and by touch.

Her tongue dried up as he gathered her hair gently to waft it down her back, instinctively moving it out of the way without her having to tell him, then settled the baby against her bosom. It was so…domestic and tranquil and a host of other things she shouldn't be wishing could continue.

This fairy-tale land Desmond had dropped her into was temporary. It couldn't be anything else, especially when he wasn't offering her more than his home and his bed. Especially when she was already having such a difficult time focusing on biology, the first love of her life. At best, she might have another few weeks of having her body worshipped in Desmond's bed, but he'd never unbend enough to want a permanent third person in his son's life.

That wasn't what she wanted either, never mind that she could easily get carried away with a fantasy about what that looked like. Fantasy—hell, it looked a lot like this, with Conner in her arms and Desmond doting on her because he'd fallen madly in love.

Lunacy. She'd never dreamed of a man falling in love with her and handing her the moon. Not once.

Until now.

After father and baby left, McKenna lost the ability to do anything other than stare off into space and replay the memory of this morning in bed, when she'd finally had the opportunity to burn images of Desmond's body into her mind. She couldn't decide if the dark was better because she had to feel her way around him or if light was better because she could watch him in the throes of passion.

If Desmond could be believed, he would give her the opportunity to do both. Every night. For how long? Until he kicked her out of his life and the baby's?

The idea of sleeping with him until then was ridiculous, a ripe situation for her to mess up and start caring for him far more deeply than she already did. The little hooks in her heart were going to hurt like hell when he finally ripped them out. She'd already been ten kinds of a fool for letting things go as far as they had.

Best thing would be to get some healthy distance. She was way overdue to visit her parents, who'd come by the hospital briefly to check on her after the birth but otherwise had stayed out of her decision to breast-feed the baby she'd given up. Who better to provide solace than the people who cared about her most?

Before she could change her mind, she slipped her phone from her bedside table and texted Desmond that she was going out, shoving back the guilt that welled higher with each letter under her thumbs. Yeah, she was intruding and forcing him to respond to an electronic communiqué he would likely hate. But seeing him in person would just give him an opportunity to ensnare her more firmly in his web of pleasure.

Desmond immediately texted her back.

I'll have the limo driver waiting for you in the roundabout at the front steps in five minutes.

She nearly groaned. So not necessary. And so ostentatious to arrive like the lady of the manor, wheeling through the middle of the place she'd grown up, especially given that a lot of the residents in the community shunned cars. But she didn't want to seem petty so she sent him back a thank-you and changed clothes, scurrying out of the house before Desmond said he could easily pack up the baby and accompany her.

She was afraid she'd agree. And allowing tagalongs wouldn't give her the distance she sorely needed.

Her pretend family dominated her thoughts as the limo cut through the swath of trees surrounding Desmond's property. This marked the first occasion she'd left the house since moving in with Desmond, which could well be the whole problem. Regular outings into the real world *should* have been a daily part of her regime. At the very least, it would have created more of a delineation between her and the Pierce males.

Desmond and Conner were the real family, no moms need apply. She'd married the man solely for convenience. It was an easy way to avoid the legal tangle of receiving a fully paid medical degree via a divorce settlement, yet, so far, nothing about their relationship felt convenient or easy. It felt like a slippery precipice with nothing to grab on to once she inevitably lost her footing.

Oddly enough, it had only just occurred to her that

she could legally adopt Desmond's last name, too, if she so chose. There was literally nothing stopping her other than the paperwork hassle times two, because she'd surely end up back at whatever office did that sort of thing to change it again when Desmond whipped out his pen to make the divorce final.

Though no one could force her to give it up, if she did do something as crazy as change it in the first place. Desmond didn't have all the power, whether he liked that reality or not.

The limo was plush, with leather seats that smelled divine and a small bar built into the sidewall that held glasses and a tub of ice with bottles of water stuck deep down in the cubes. Nice touch. She still couldn't drink alcohol while breast-feeding, a sacrifice she didn't mind since she wasn't much of a drinker anyway. Desmond's attention to detail warmed her far more than it should have.

Once the driver left Astoria, he veered inland and the forest swallowed the car. Long, dark shadows kept the limo in partial sunlight for the rest of the drive to Harmony Gardens on the other side of the Clatsop Forest where her parents lived.

Yes, she definitely should have done this much earlier. The quiet hush of the trees bled through her soul, calming her, filling her with peace. The forest had been here long before she was born. It persevered, growing and thriving despite all the forces working against it.

She would, too.

Her mother waited for her in the small yard of the clapboard house near the center of Harmony Gardens. It had been McKenna's grandfather's house before he passed and her parents had moved in to care for him a month before her twelfth birthday. Grandfather's long battle with cancer had kept him in and out of different healing centers until he'd taken his final breath in the back bedroom. While a terrible ordeal for everyone, it had sparked the kernel of McKenna's dream to be a doctor.

The care Grandfather had received had been loving, patient. But ultimately ineffective. She'd begged him to see a medical doctor, to try radiation. *Not for me*, he'd insisted as McKenna's mother took him to yet another shaman or crystologist. Would the cancer have killed him even with western medicine? No way to know.

But McKenna could surely replicate the kindness the alternative medicine practitioners had demonstrated as she sought to heal people with the methods *she* trusted. No one else had her unique mix of drive, determination and a husband with deep pockets.

The plan would have been flawless if Conner hadn't developed formula allergies. If she hadn't started to feel things for Desmond that she shouldn't.

The driver parked near the house and swept open the back door of the limo, holding out his hand to help McKenna from the seat. She smiled her thanks, stepping back in time as she turned to follow the trail of worn brick pavers leading to her mother.

"My sweet darling," her mother crooned as she embraced McKenna.

Love enveloped her instantly, soothing her raw nerves and drawing her into a place where everything in her world made sense.

"You didn't have to hang around outside," she chided her mother gently. "I know how to knock."

"I couldn't sit still. I haven't seen you in months, except for thirty minutes in that dreadful hospital." Her mother's long, dark braid danced as she shook her head.

It was a rare occasion that the braid, now shot with a few silver strands, wasn't hanging down her back.

A tinge of grief gripped McKenna's stomach as she realized her mother was aging. Of course she was. Though in her early fifties, Rebecca Moore still looked forty, with beautiful skin that had started to sport small crinkles at the eyes and thin lines around her mouth. She looked exactly the same as she had the last time McKenna had seen her barely two months ago, after Conner had been born.

This was just the first time McKenna had a benchmark. Giving birth had done that somehow, where six years of school had not. One year had blended into the next and, finally, she'd graduated. A baby, on the other hand, grew and aged alongside you—or at least that was how it was supposed to work. McKenna's baby wouldn't come visit her when she was in her early fifties and carry along with him all of the memories of watching him grow up, of raising him, loving him. Seeing his first steps, first lost tooth, first date.

A tear slipped down McKenna's cheek before she could catch it.

"Oh, honey." Her mother clucked. "Come inside and let me get you a drink so you can tell me what's bothering you so badly that you came all the way down here to see me."

So much for trying to keep her inner turmoil in check. But gaining some clarity was the whole reason she was there. Why not tell her mom everything?

McKenna followed her mother into the small, ancient house. Her parents had done their best to preserve the interior in a snapshot of the way Grandfather had kept it. His old chair still sat by the fireplace where he'd spent many hours warding off the chill that had constantly haunted him in his last days. Photographs of her mom and dad as kids playing together lined the walls. They'd known each other their whole lives, just like many of the couples who comprised the community. Growing up, McKenna had always understood that the beliefs of many of those who resided in Harmony Gardens didn't reflect societal norms, thus they tended to stay insulated.

She'd rocked the boat by leaving. Embracing her dream of being a doctor. Moving to Portland. Having a baby and giving him up.

"I know you don't approve of my choices..." she began, but already her mother shook her head, braid bouncing against her shoulders.

"That's not what's bothering you." Her mother handed her a glass of water and pulled McKenna onto the couch that had seen many years of wear, most of it happy, and some tears. Like now. How did her mother see through her so easily?

"But I need you to hear this," McKenna said as the next tear slipped down her cheek. "You don't seem to understand how important being a doctor is to me."

Her mother slipped an arm around McKenna's shoulders, holding on tight like she used to when warding off the boogeymen when McKenna had a nightmare about creatures creeping out from the surrounding forest and standing outside her window.

"I've never questioned your commitment to following your dreams," she said. "What I've tried to do is help you see that there are other factors to consider."

"Like having lots of babies is a factor I should consider?" Frustrated all at once, McKenna shoved off the couch and out of her mother's reach.

"No," her mother countered calmly. "Like the fact that sometimes one is all you get. You know your father and

I weren't able to have more children. We wanted more, desperately. Not because you weren't enough. You're amazing and special. We wanted to give you brothers and sisters."

"And do your part to populate the community." It wasn't a secret that her parents had long held that belief. Children were not only a happy gift from God, according to them, but Harmony Gardens sustained itself by every member pitching in. The more members, the better.

But McKenna felt crappy bringing it up when the sole reason was to detract from the aching hole that had just opened up in her chest.

Sometimes one is all you get.

Was that her fate, too? Conner could be her only child. The endometriosis that had rendered her mother infertile could very well be in McKenna's DNA, too, waiting to strike after she'd birthed her first baby. That would be now.

She shook her head, shoving back the wave of emotion. "It doesn't matter. I don't want children."

The sentiment rang so much hollower than it had in the past. While she didn't want the nebulous term that encompassed "children," she couldn't include Conner in that statement. He was a baby that already existed, one she never should have come to care for.

Her mother's eyes softened. "Sit with me. Let's talk about that for a minute."

Warily, McKenna complied. "You can't talk me into wanting children. I made a deal."

"Yes, let's not dwell on that, shall we? You've made your choice and I understand that you've signed agreements that you'll never have contact with the baby, which by default means we'll never know our grandchild. What's done is done." Folding her hand around McKenna's, her mother squeezed, gracing her with compassion she didn't feel she deserved all at once.

"I…" She'd never considered that she was punishing her parents as well as herself by giving up Conner.

"Not dwelling on it," her mother reminded her. "Instead let's talk about why you don't want to have children."

"Because women don't have the same choices as men," she burst out. "Especially not in a place like Harmony. They have their first baby at eighteen or nineteen and, before you know it, they have nothing more defining them than being a mother. They're sucked dry with no time or energy left over to make a difference."

Quietly her mother stroked her hand. "The point is that having children is making a difference in their minds, and that's *their* choice. You never saw that. Nor have you recognized that some people do have careers and children. With you, it's always been either-or."

"Having children while going to medical school is not an option," McKenna countered. She could barely take two classes and maintain her sanity with a baby and a sexy man in the house. Not to mention that online classes that counted toward a medical degree were few and far between. "Besides, it doesn't matter. That's not an option."

"And that's the problem." Her mother nodded sagely as two more tears slipped down McKenna's cheek. "I was worried this might happen. You're so matter-of-fact about your decisions and you don't honor your feelings enough."

"Emotions are not a good thing to base decisions on." So easy to say. Thus far, it had been easy to do. She'd always had a practical nature, which was part of the reason being a doctor appealed to her.

How could she have predicted that she'd ever have so many impossible dreams racing through her chest, ones that hurt when she contemplated them?

"You're right." McKenna shut her eyes for a moment, willing back the next flood of tears. They were right there, threatening to well up as she forced herself to reconcile what her mother was telling her. "The problem isn't that I feel a certain way about anything. It's that I don't have a choice."

"You don't like not having choices."

This was not a new conversation. They'd had this argument many times, especially when she'd first sprung the concept of being a surrogate on her parents and they'd accused her of picking this option deliberately to thumb her nose at the concepts they'd long held dear. "That's n—"

It was true.

She knew it was true. She liked having control over her own life. Why was she about to argue that fact? Because she'd just realized she had more in common with Desmond than she'd credited?

It was the whole reason she didn't appreciate his attempts at manipulation. Perceived attempts, she reminded herself. She didn't know his motivation for being so helpful when it came to breast-feeding or in being so greedy for her pleasure in bed either, for that matter.

But it smacked of control and that she would not tolerate. Especially when he'd already made it so clear that he insisted on absolute control when it came to Conner. Fine. That was set in stone and she couldn't change it now. But she did not have to let him control anything else.

She should demand that Desmond hire a nanny. Today. She'd avoided that subject because of all the waffling going on in her heart about leaving. No more. Not only did she need a nanny in the house as soon as possible, she wanted a date on the calendar for the divorce. That was how she could maintain control over her choices.

"I see your wheels turning," her mother said with a small smile. "Keep in mind that I love you as I say this. The world is not black-and-white. You tend to think of your choices that way, when in reality, things are not so easily put into your either-or buckets. Especially not when you start to have feelings for someone."

She scowled. "I don't have feelings for anyone. What are you talking about?"

"That you want to feel like you have control over your emotions and, sweetie, it just doesn't work that way. When you meet the one, you don't have a choice. You just…fall."

"In love?" she squawked. That wasn't what was happening to her. It couldn't be. "I'm not—I mean, okay, Desmond is kind and unexpectedly…"

Hot. Wickedly talented in bed. His mouth alone should have had a warning label. None of that seemed to be the kind of thing you said to your mother. Neither could she actually admit that her mother was right.

The knowing look on her mother's face said she'd already figured it out. "Go home to your husband, McKenna, and give the unexpected a chance. You might find that you have more choices than you originally thought."

But the one choice she desperately needed wasn't open to her. She could not choose to stop falling in love with Desmond. That was a done deal.

Nine

Despite promising himself he wouldn't listen for the crunch of gravel under the limo tires, Desmond did it anyway. So he knew the instant McKenna had returned from wherever she'd gone. Finally.

He'd missed her. The house had felt empty without her in it, as if it had been drained of something vital. She'd been gone for four hours and it had felt like a lifetime. He was in serious trouble here, with little to no idea how to put the final threads in the fabric of the family he wanted. But nothing would stop him from trying.

She came inside and stopped short when she saw him hanging around like an idiot in the foyer, pretending to play with Conner, as if the kid didn't have a nursery, a recreation room and maybe five other places more hospitable to a baby than a drafty open area near the front door.

Her smile lit on the son they shared and Desmond soaked it in, enchanted by the way she filled his space with her presence and still mystified why the invasion didn't bother him. It should. Not one but two people were in his sanctuary. He liked them here. And she'd been responsible for both.

"Hi," he said and it sounded as lame out loud as it had in his head. The other stuff he'd practiced dried up as her gaze skittered away from him.

Something wasn't right. His senses picked up on it instantly.

"Hey," she said.

A dark shadow moved through his consciousness as he internalized her response. He tried to ignore it. "Did you have a good time?"

"Sure."

That was supposed to be an opening for her to tell him about her day, mention where she'd gone.

"I—"

"I'm tired, Desmond." She wouldn't look at him. "I'm going to take a nap before dinner."

He let her go and tried not to stress about her mood. After all the amazing things they'd shared, it was frustrating that she didn't want to open up to him. He did *alone* better than anyone, but he'd found a reason not to be and would stake his life on the fact that she'd felt something binding them together just as strongly as he had.

For some reason, she wasn't engaging.

Without any more answers, he retreated to his workshop after dinner—which McKenna did not eat with him—and played with Conner. He put the boy to bed and fiddled around with one of the analog switches in his robotic humanoid, but his mind refused to participate in what was largely a distraction anyway.

The computer dinged to alert him that McKenna had

come online. It didn't take but a quarter of a second for him to envision her sitting at her desk studying, brow furrowed in concentration as she swept that gorgeous fall of hair behind her back. He'd like to visit her again, offer to help with her homework, but given her earlier reticence he had a feeling it would be a short conversation.

Of course there was only one way to find out.

His footfalls outside her open door must have alerted her to his presence because she'd already turned the chair a half twist as he drew even with the threshold. Maybe she'd been anticipating his arrival, remembering the last time he'd come to her room to help with her chemistry problems.

They'd resolved all of them, one way or another. But his favorite was still that first orgasm, when she'd come so fast he couldn't wait to do it again.

"I'm glad you're here," she said with a tentative smile and motioned him inside. "I think we should talk."

That was probably the last thing on his mind. And should be the last thing on hers. Lots of work to do here if talking was the first thing she wanted to do. Casually, he leaned on the edge of the desk to disguise how tense his body had grown with the effort to not sweep her into his arms. "About your homework?"

Seeing her in the flesh still kicked him in the gut, but the feeling had so many more teeth now, slicing open nerve endings and fanning through his blood with sensual heat that only she could tame.

Her gaze locked with his and she swallowed. But didn't look away, like she had earlier. "No, um… Let's start with Conner. That nanny-finding service is really falling down on the job. Maybe you should hire another one?"

"I can take care of my son," he said gruffly, still reeling from her nearness.

He'd made love to her twice just that morning. How many times would be enough to still this raging need inside?

"I know." She bit her lip, eyeing him as he moved a few centimeters closer. He couldn't help it. She smelled so good. "But the nanny will do more than just care for Conner. I feel like we've had this conversation a hundred times. I need to start figuring out how to wean so I can move back to Portland."

Well, that put things in perspective. If he'd wondered whether she'd ever thought about sticking around, he didn't have to wonder any longer. Even after last night, she still couldn't wait to be rid of him.

He needed to put some more icing on the cake.

"It's barely been two months," he countered and somehow kept the hitch out of his voice. "We agreed the baby would likely need you for a few more months yet. Are you feeling restless? I'll have a car delivered tomorrow so you can come and go at will."

She blew out a breath. "That's very generous but—"

"I seem to recall a few other ways you've enjoyed my generosity recently." He picked up her hand and held it to his lips, inhaling her scent. "I'm thinking of expanding on that. Right now."

"Oh, um…" Her eyes widened as he sucked one of her fingers into his mouth. "That wasn't what I wanted to talk about."

"So talk," he said around her finger and laved at the tip. "Don't mind me."

Her eyelids fluttered closed as he mouthed his way across her palm and nibbled at her wrist. "It's hard to think when you're doing that."

"Hint. That means you like it," he whispered and concentrated on her elbow where his tongue got a groan out of her that hardened him instantly.

"That's the problem. I don't want to like it. I want to talk about how we're going to get the baby to a point where I can leave—"

"McKenna." It was a wonder he got that out around the vise that had clamped around his throat. "Stop talking about leaving. Let the future take care of itself. In the meantime, if you're unhappy, say so. That's the only way I can fix it."

Her hesitation bled through him, ruffling the pit of fire near his groin. "I'm not unhappy. Don't be ridiculous. I'm just...concerned. I don't see any kind of exit plan and—"

"No exit plan. We can come up with one later." *Or never.* "Right now, I want to enjoy you. And help you enjoy yourself. Let me."

"I don't know what you're asking me to do." She shook her head, gripping his hand tighter instead of slipping free like he'd have expected.

Crap, he was botching this. He needed more time to figure out how to persuade her. Except she'd been so quiet all afternoon. There was no telling how long he had before she'd shut down again and, besides, he wasn't much of a verbal dancer.

"McKenna." He pulled her into his arms with a growl, determined to get her over whatever was going through her head that was keeping them apart. "I want you in my bed. I want to watch you care for my son. The shape of what I want is already there. What it's called is a question for another day."

He already knew what to call it—his family. The vision in his head would shatter without the integral third she represented. Somehow he had to communicate what was in his mind and his heart whether he had all the right words or not. There was only one surefire way to do that in his experience.

Before McKenna could blink, Des swept her up in his arms and carried her out of her room. Her gorgeous hair draped over his shoulder and he couldn't wait to get his hands on it.

Breathlessly, she sputtered, "Wh-what are you doing?"

"Taking you to my room," he growled. "Where you belong. You sleep there from now on, where I can properly take care of you."

"Or what?" she challenged as her pulse picked up, beating hard against his fingertips. It was a clear indication he'd gotten her attention.

But because he wasn't a complete beast, he laid her out gently on the bed and stepped back, giving her plenty of room to breathe, bolt or bare herself to him, pending how well he'd gauged the swing in her mood. "There's no 'or what.' Give me two minutes to convince you this is what you want."

Arms crossed, she contemplated him, her eyelids at half-mast. But that wasn't enough to conceal the intrigue and excitement his challenge had stimulated. "While I'm dressed?"

"Hell, no, you won't be dressed," he shot back. "The point is that I want you in my bed *naked*. I want you to be here when I go to sleep, when I wake up. When it's time to nurse the baby and all the times in between. I—"

As he choked on his own emotion, her gaze softened and she held out her hand. "Come here. Instead of slinging ultimatums and deals around, lie down. *Dressed*. Talk to me."

That, he could do. He stretched out next to her and laid his head on his bent arm as she caressed his temple, threading his hair through her fingers soothingly. It wasn't sexual. It was…nice.

"I don't know how to do this," he confessed. This was barely *his* room, let alone hers. But he knew he wanted to be in it. With her. She brought his entire house to life just by being there.

"I know. This isn't what I expected either." Tenderness bled through him as she let her hand trail down his jaw to rest against his neck. "Just cool your jets for a minute and stop trying to manipulate me with sex."

"That's not what…" Yeah. It was exactly what he'd been trying to do. Give-a-woman-enough-orgasms-and-she-stopped-looking-for-the-door kind of philosophy. That clearly wasn't working. "What can I do to convince you that I genuinely want to spend time with you?"

"Tell me." Her expression warmed. "I like to hear the truth. I also like to have choices."

As insights went, that was a big one. "I'm sensing you don't mean a choice between making you come with my fingers or my mouth."

She arched a brow. "Well, I can't lie. That's not really a choice because my answer is always both. No, I mean the fact that you don't like to give me any control when it comes to things like hiring a nanny. I worry that sex will cloud the issues."

Nodding, he filtered through what she was saying, her nonverbal cues and how to reconcile all of that with the aching need to keep her by his side. She clearly wasn't balking at his desire to sleep with her, just the fact that he'd been grasping the strings of his life too tightly.

Control was his default. It shielded his vulnerabilities. But she was saying he had to give or she'd walk.

"So hiring a nanny will help you feel like you've got choices?"

"Well, sure. Because it means you're not so stuck in your control-freak land." She smiled to soften the sting of her terminology but, honestly, she wasn't off base. The thought of losing her hurt far worse than being told the truth about himself.

"I don't want to hire a nanny." He held up a finger as her expression darkened. "But not because I'm trying to control you. Because I should be the one taking care of my son. I have a problem connecting with people. I don't want that to affect our relationship. If I'm all he knows, he'll come to me for a Band-Aid."

Her warm hands came up to cup his jaw as she re-settled on her pillow much closer to him than she had been. "Oh, honey. I didn't mean for that to be such a defining moment in your decisions as a father when I pointed that out."

"But it was. And it should have been." Because it felt natural and right, he tucked an arm around her waist, drawing her body up against his. They were still fully clothed but their position was by far the most intimate thing he'd ever done with anyone. "I needed to hear that. I've been reading up on how to wean a baby with formula allergies. I'm going to help you."

He should have started long before now but, as always, she saw him more clearly than he saw himself.

Something raw and tender exploded in the depths of her eyes. "Really? You'd do that for me?"

"Well, yes. Of course."

The gruff note in his voice wasn't due to uncertainty like usual. It was pure emotion. She was softening; he could feel it. Feel them binding together in this quiet moment that had nothing to do with sex. All because he'd loosened his grip. That was as much of a defining moment as anything else.

He needed McKenna to push him like this, to help him see that giving a woman choices didn't mean she'd immediately stomp on his emotions.

The sweet kiss she laid on his lips was just as raw and tender, sweeping through him with the force of a tidal wave, clear-cutting a path through his body straight to his heart.

"McKenna," he murmured against her lips, and she burrowed closer with a soft sigh, wedging a thigh between his as she deepened the kiss.

Everything shifted in the space of a moment. Urgency built, a yearning to touch, to revel, to feel.

To experience. Not to claim.

Reverently he took great handfuls of her hair. She moaned as he levered her head back to allow him access to taste her throat, the hollow behind her ear, her lobe, anything he could put his mouth on. Then he ran out of skin.

Stripping her became an act of adoration. Each button slipped free of its housing, revealing another slice of her, and he christened what he'd uncovered with a kiss. She shifted restlessly, her desire mounting so fast his head spun.

When he spread the fabric of her shirt wide, she arched her back, pushing closer to his mouth, so he indulged them both, laving at her exposed flesh and dipping under the fabric of her bra as he worked at getting her pants off. It was a much bigger trick when she was lying on the bed and he was facedown in her breasts, a problem he didn't mind solving the old-fashioned way—brute strength. He picked her up by the hips and tore off the offending garments until she was fully bared.

He took a moment to let his gaze sweep over her, lingering at her breasts, hard nipples taut and gorgeous.

Her lungs audibly hitched as he reached out to stroke. Looked like she wasn't of a mind to bolt or breathe. That worked for him.

Ripping out of his clothes in record time, he resettled next to her on the bed, stroking whatever he could reach and murmuring nonsense about how beautiful she was. His brain was a tangle of wants, needs and absolutes, all of which began and ended with McKenna. The more he stroked, the higher the urgency climbed until he was nearly writhing as much as she was.

Because he couldn't hold out much longer, he knelt to take her over the crest the first time, gratified that he could sense exactly where to put his tongue to wring the tightest, strongest orgasm from her. What a total high to discover he could use his empathy in such a pleasurable way.

She gasped and moaned her way down from the peak, eagerly collapsing against his body as he pulled her into his arms.

"More," she croaked, and he couldn't hear that enough.

But this time he needed to be with her, soaring alongside. In a flash, he had himself sheathed and pushing inside to bathe in the bliss of her body as she accepted him to the hilt, so hot and ready for him that it took his breath.

"Yes," she cried and wound her hips in a slow circle, drawing him deeper still until he was lost in the sensation. "You feel amazing."

That didn't begin to describe the way they mated spiritually as well as physically. But he wanted more and wasn't going to stop until he got it.

"Imagine how much better this would feel if we didn't have to use condoms," he risked saying aloud.

He wanted to spill his seed in her, to see if he could sense the moment when she conceived. They'd hold hands as they took a pregnancy test together, waiting with breathless anticipation to confirm what he already knew in his soul would be a plus sign.

The ghosts that had haunted him since Lacey would finally vanish.

McKenna half laughed and let her head tip back as he nuzzled her neck. "Yeah, if this is how the next few months are going to be, I should definitely see about a more permanent form of birth control."

Cold invaded his chest and he willed it back. He had months to convince her of what was happening here but, for the first time, everything seemed to be falling into place. No longer would he live in fear of his family being ripped apart by forces beyond his control.

He changed the subject by hefting her thigh higher on his hip and driving her into the heavens a second time before following her into the white light of release.

McKenna was his and he was not letting her go.

Days bled into a week and Desmond waited for McKenna to come up with another argument against living as husband and wife. But she didn't mention leaving again. At night she slept in his bed and during Conner's naps she sat in the corner of his workshop with her laptop, blazing through her online classes brilliantly.

It helped that he was right there to help, cheerfully stopping whatever he was doing—usually watching her out of the corner of his eye—to answer a question or to call up a resource from his knowledge bank.

By the middle of the second week Des didn't know what to call this euphoria. The only term he could think of was *happiness*. That had never been a goal of his and he'd never have thought it would be the result of getting what he'd asked for. But what else could this be?

True to his word, Desmond bought McKenna a breast pump and they worked together to get Conner used to taking his meals from a bottle. The baby's pediatrician proved a great help, suggesting they alternate a hypoallergenic formula with breast milk and gauge how he responded.

They kept careful watch, took notes, switched formulas as Conner reacted to the elements found in one or the other. McKenna hated the process, sometimes crying at night in Desmond's arms as the formula caused hives to break out on the baby's skin or he constantly spit up.

"I'm the most selfish person on the planet," she wailed, her distress eating through Des as he held her, stroking her hair, forehead, whatever he could get his hands on, though nothing stemmed the tide of her bleakness.

"No. This is an important step for him," he told her, quoting the doctor. "This is not just something we're doing so you can stop breast-feeding. We have to know what he's allergic to as he may have sensitivity to milk and soy his whole life."

Her tears soaked his shoulder, running down into the mattress below. "But I'm making him deal with this while he's still so tiny. I could breast-feed for a year. Two. People do it all the time."

"Sure you could. But at what cost?"

What kind of hell was this where he was forced into the role of convincing her that weaning was the right thing for everyone? Once she didn't have to feed the baby any longer, she could leave whenever she wanted. But he was slowly conceding that she needed options. He had to believe that when push came to shove, she'd choose Desmond and Conner. The concessions he'd made internally to get himself to this point were enormous. And so worth it.

"Sweetheart, listen to me." He levered up her chin with one finger until she met his gaze. "We're going to get through this. Together. I promised you."

She nodded and sighed, wiping at her leaking eyes. "Take my mind off it. Right now."

Her busy hands made short work of removing the drawstring pants he wore at night, leaving no room for him to misinterpret what she intended for him to do to grant her oblivion.

That was one thing he never minded letting her control. "Gladly."

In the morning they started all over again with the baby. Finally they settled on a rice-based formula that proved the least problematic.

After the third time feeding him without a reaction, McKenna glanced up at Desmond, her eyes bright as she held Conner to her shoulder, his little head listing against hers as she burped him. "I think this is it."

He nodded, afraid to upset the status quo with something as irreverent as speech. What would he say that could mark such a momentous, emotionally difficult occasion?

"It's kind of hard to believe I'm done," she said with a catch in her voice.

Conner made one of his baby noises and Des retrieved him from his mother in the same manner as he had almost since the moment of his son's birth. Only this time he did it to cover his own melancholy reaction to the passage of a ritual he'd grown to love.

Watching her breast-feed had been holy and beautiful. He'd never imagined he'd mourn the loss of it and regret that the last time he'd get to experience it had already happened. He'd have commemorated the occasion, or savored it longer, if he'd realized.

It was too late now. They'd reached the goal they'd set for themselves. Now McKenna could make a choice to stay with a clear head and no sense of obligation. He couldn't contemplate another scenario.

He cleared his throat. "You were fantastic. The whole time. So amazing. You sacrificed so much for our son. I—"

"Your son," she corrected. "Now that he's weaned, he can be totally your son again. I wasn't going to bring it up so soon, but while we're on the subject…let's talk about the divorce."

A roaring sound in Desmond's ears cut off the rest of her speech. "What are you talking about?"

She recoiled, her mouth still open. "Our agreement. The baby is weaned. The new semester starts in a couple of weeks. The timing is perfect for me to register. But I can't until I get the settlement money."

The baby squeaked as Desmond hefted him higher on his shoulder. Before he could have this conversation, Conner came first. He settled the baby into the bouncy seat that served as his primary residence when he wasn't asleep or being held. The stuffed giraffe hanging from the center bar caught the baby's attention and he kicked at it, his eyes tracking the trajectory of his foot.

When Des thought he could be a touch more civil, he turned back to McKenna who was still sitting in the rocker that she'd moved from her former bedroom to the one she now shared with him. He'd practiced how to approach the subject of her tuition but, honestly, he'd talked himself out of believing she'd bring it up.

The shock of her decision still hadn't faded. He swallowed as he absorbed her taciturn expression. Had the last few months meant nothing to her? He'd been falling into her, falling into the possibilities and he'd have sworn she was too. He couldn't be so out of touch that he'd mistaken that. No way was he alone in feeling these big, bright emotions.

"We have an agreement, Desmond." Her quiet voice cut through him.

"I'm aware," he said more curtly than he'd have liked, but his entire body had frozen. "I had hoped you'd reconsider."

"Reconsider what?" Her mouth dropped open as understanding dawned. "You thought I'd reconsider becoming a doctor?"

"No, of course not. I meant reconsider the divorce."

"You're not making any sense. Our agreement was that you'd file for the divorce once I gave birth. Then the formula allergy happened, but I always expected you to come through with your part of the promise." The tight cross of her arms over her still ample bosom drew his attention and that's when he noticed her hands were shaking. "Conner doesn't need me anymore. I have to go."

"I need you!" he burst out before thinking better of how such a statement gave her power to cut him open. "What do you think we've been doing here but building something permanent?"

Her eyelids fluttered closed. "No," she whispered. "We can't. That's not the deal."

"Screw the deal. I want you to stay." *I want you to feel the things I feel.*

"Forever? That's impossible!" She leaped to her feet as Conner started crying. "Now the baby is upset. I can't stand it when he's upset."

She couldn't stand it? The twin streams of black distress—Conner's and McKenna's—sank barbed hooks into Desmond's consciousness, wringing him out like a wet rag. Conflict was not his forte, especially when he hadn't been expecting it, and he did not handle it well.

McKenna hurried to the bouncy seat and scooped up the baby, cradling him as if she never meant to let him go. Didn't she see that she belonged here, holding Conner, caring for him? Didn't she see how much control Desmond had conceded to her, laying himself bare?

"I'm going to take Conner to Mrs. Elliot," she said firmly. "And then we're going to finish this conversation once and for all."

She wasn't gone long enough for his empathy to settle or his temper. The words in his head refused to gel into coherent sentences. He was losing her and he couldn't grab on any tighter.

"You can't leave," he told her grimly as she stopped a half foot over the threshold of his bedroom.

"Or what? You'll tie me to the bed?"

She let her head drop into her hands and her shoulders quaked for a beat. But then she lifted her face to reveal the deepest agony he'd ever seen. It bled through him, nearly crippling him with her grief.

"You can't keep me here. Don't you see how it's killing me to leave Conner? Sometimes I think everyone would be happier if I gave up my dreams. Everyone except me. I can't be a mother and a doctor. It's not in my makeup. I have to choose. And you have to give me that choice."

"I've given you choices," he growled even as he sensed that what she was saying was the rawest form of truth. These were things she felt deeply. Just as clearly, he got the sense she did care about him. Not enough to stay, though, and it was killing him. "Lots of them. This is not the same situation as before, when you needed to feel like you had some measure of control—"

"Yes it is!" Clearly bewildered, she shook her head. "Yes, you gave me choices with Conner and I appreciate them. But you were the one who held me when I cried and said it was important that I wean. That if I kept breast-feeding, it would have too high a cost. The cost would have been my medical degree. I thought you knew that. Agreed."

"The cost was to Conner," he stormed as the barb she'd sank into his heart cleaved through it with so much pain that it was too hard to sort out whether it was hers or his. "There was never a point where I thought we were weaning so you could leave us. I thought—" *You were happy here.*

That she was falling for him as he was falling for her. Hell, there was no falling left to do. He'd opened himself emotionally, sometimes against his will. Though, to be honest, the dominoes had started lining up the moment he'd spied her for the first time in that hospital bed.

"I gave birth to Conner for *you*. I wanted to give you a family. But that's all I can give." Wide-eyed, she surveyed him, her expression so stricken he nearly yanked her into his arms so he could soothe her. "I didn't expect you to be kind and amazing. It's hard for me to leave you, too. But this is what I have to do, Des."

She'd never called him that before. It was almost an endearment. In the final hour she'd conceded that she did have feelings for him. But her feelings didn't seem to matter.

"What do you want?" he whispered and bit back the flood of words he wished he could say. *I love you* being first and foremost. But he couldn't stand the thought of stripping himself even more emotionally bare.

"The choice," she answered simply. "File for divorce."

No. His soul cried out the word but he couldn't force it out of his throat.

"Don't you get it?" she continued when he didn't immediately agree. "You've supported me for over a year with a golden handcuff. I have nothing on my own. If you don't grant me the divorce, you've simply transferred your need to control things from one area to another. It's so hard for me to make this choice. I don't need the additional complexity of not being given one."

He nodded once. How ironic that his greatest life lesson would come at his own hands. He'd structured the agreement expressly so she had no control and, thus, no ability to hurt him. Instead she was following the agreement to the letter—and tearing him apart at the same time.

"You will still choose to become a doctor."

It was inevitable. Final. Incentives, orgasms, choices—his heart—none of this had been enough. If only he could lie to himself, he might be able to salvage the situation. But in the end, he knew the truth: he had to give her what she'd requested.

She nodded. "I have an obligation to myself. I've been working on saying goodbye this whole time. You have to let me do that."

Once again McKenna was pushing him out of his comfort zone, forcing him to look in the mirror. The family, the connections he'd been building, weren't a beautiful creation but a mirage. And if he didn't let her go, he'd be the monster instead of Dr. Frankenstein.

Ten

The university had walking paths, one of which ran right behind the little house Desmond had bought for McKenna. She'd expected to live in the dorm but he'd insisted she'd want the peace and quiet, so she'd accepted the key from the Realtor and kept her mouth shut when furniture arrived via a large van with the name of an exclusive store stenciled on the side.

This was what she'd asked for. Maybe not the part where the contents of the small house were worth more than her parents made in a year. But she did like the French country style that took shape around her, especially the functional desk she'd directed the movers to put in the dining room that would act as her office, where she'd study.

She had zero plans to entertain. Medical school was as demanding and difficult as she'd envisioned. Desmond had prepaid for her entire degree, citing the divorce might take too long to be finalized, thus he might as well pay for everything now.

One nice benefit to the house being off campus: she didn't feel compelled to take part in any of the campus activities and instead could focus on her class work, which she did, every night.

After three or four days she forced herself to drive to the grocery store in the practical Honda that Desmond had given her with express instructions to take it somewhere to have maintenance done every five thousand miles. Since she drove it less than ten miles a week, it would take about ninety years to reach that first milestone.

Of course, every time she got behind the wheel, she thought about driving it to Astoria and straight up the drive to the remote mansion along the Columbia River. What she'd do when she got there, she had no idea. This was her life now. The one she'd planned, envisioned, fought for.

The life she'd left behind at Desmond's was not hers, not real, not possible. How dare he act like that was a choice, like she could just stay there in the lap of luxury and let him take care of her while she gave up her dreams? While she ached to understand how he really felt about her without all the fantastic sex to muddle things?

The complications that had always been there had gotten worse. Mostly because Desmond had climbed into her heart and taken up residence when she wasn't looking. She had no idea what to do with that big, frightening reality.

What if she stuck around and the way she felt about him got bigger, scarier, more painful? Then she'd have no choices and a broken heart when he got bored with her and *then* filed the divorce papers. They were already signed, had been since before she'd conceived. The only thing he had to do was to take them to the court and it would be done. All part and parcel of their agreement. He had always had all of the power and no apparent qualms about throwing it around.

She'd demanded the choice and when he'd given it to her, she'd taken the opportunity to leave. It was the only way she could stay sane. After all, she ached to be with both Desmond and Conner past the point of reason, and it was killing her to be apart from them both, regardless of how necessary it was.

McKenna walked to her 9:00 a.m. pain management course on Monday, marking the first time in several days rain wasn't falling in a continual downpour. She'd tucked an umbrella into her bag because it was still Portland. Rain was predictable.

When she got to the building, one of the many guys in her class stood by the door. She started to brush past him but he stopped her with a nice smile.

"McKenna, right?"

Uh-oh. Was she being hit on? With Desmond, it was always completely obvious what had been on his mind, probably because it had been on hers, too. She missed that, missed his straightforwardness and wicked way with his hands. The ever-present ache in her chest got a whole lot worse as she drowned in memories.

And the guy was still smiling at her.

"Yes. I'm McKenna." She scouted her memory for his name but came up blank. There was a sea of faces on campus and none of them stuck out.

"It's Mark," he supplied easily with another nice smile, and she really wished she could smile back but she didn't want to encourage him.

"So, listen…" he continued. "I was wondering if you had some time this afternoon to go over the notes from last week. I missed a lecture because my daughter had an appointment."

"Oh. Um. Sure." Then what he'd said registered. "You have a daughter?"

"Yeah, she's great. My wife is a champ, taking care of her and working at the same time while I go to school. Do you have kids?"

She shook her head automatically. Conner wasn't hers and for all of Desmond's talk about keeping her around, there'd never really been any give on his part regarding that. He wasn't asking her to be his wife and his son's mother. Just the woman in his bed.

"So, about the notes?" Mark asked again, obviously interested in school not flirting. "I know it's an imposition, but I couldn't miss my daughter's appointment. It's a balance, but worth it, you know?"

No, she had no clue how someone could balance medical school and being a parent, let alone being married. "Sure, no problem."

They exchanged phone numbers and she sat through the class, half listening to the professor's long-winded lecture about chronic pain. Actually she had a pretty good idea how someone balanced medical school and life. She'd done it with Conner and her online class, with Desmond's help. And once she started thinking about how often the man she'd married had stepped up to assist her in all aspects of motherhood, classes—orgasms—she couldn't stop.

Somehow she got through the day, met up with Mark in the library to let him copy her notes, and wandered back home at the end of her last class. It had started to rain, no shock. But she didn't put up her umbrella, letting the light drizzle soak through her hair and clothes before she'd even noticed.

The phantoms she sometimes heard late at night were growing more active during the day. When she walked into the small house she could have sworn she heard Conner's baby noises wafting from the ceiling. Impossible. She shut the door and tried to care that she was dripping water all over the new throw rug covering the hardwood floor.

Her chest was on fire, aching to hold her baby, aching to be with her baby's father. But how could she stay under Desmond's thumb and never go to medical school? People who got sick like her grandfather needed an advocate in their corner. Someone to convince them that medical care in a hospital wasn't the evil they thought it was.

What choice did she really have?

Instead of sitting at her beautiful desk and working on her exhaustive list of assignments, she stripped out of her wet clothes and fell into bed, pulling the covers up to warm her chilled body. It didn't help. The cold penetrated straight to her core.

Choices. They haunted her. The ones she'd demanded. The ones she'd made.

It was the ultimate act of selfishness, wishing she could somehow have everything—the man she'd fallen in love with, the baby she'd never dreamed she'd want to keep *and* earn the medical degree she'd long believed was her path.

She slept fitfully only to wake at midnight, hot and uncomfortable under the pile of blankets. Throwing them off, she lay there naked, welcoming the cool air. No way would she go back to sleep now. And she had an assignment due in ten hours that she hadn't touched. Homework was the last thing she wanted to do. But this was the lot she'd chosen and she had to persevere.

When she booted up her laptop, the little blue icon popped up to let her know Desmond was online. Shocked, she stared at the message until it faded. He hadn't uninstalled the chat program? Had he found someone else to chat with? Also, geez. It was midnight. Was he up because he couldn't sleep? Maybe he'd been lying awake aching to hear someone else's heartbeat next to him in the bed. Doubtful. That was probably just her.

More likely Conner had woken up looking for a bottle. Oh, God. What if he was crying because he wanted his mother and was confused and frightened because she wasn't there? She had to check.

She'd clicked open the chat window and typed *hi* before fully thinking it through. If Desmond was in his workshop online, the odds were good that he wasn't taking care of Conner.

Too late now. He'd know instantly that she was messed up.

The message sat there blinking with no response and she nearly shut the program down. But then came the very cryptic return comment.

Desmond: *hi.*

Not capitalized, no punctuation. What the hell? Aliens had surely possessed the body of the man she'd married. And what was she supposed to say back? *Don't mind me, I'm just sitting here regretting everything I've ever done up to and including typing hi.*

McKenna: *Sorry to bother you.*

She nearly groaned. That had always been his line. For the first time she had the opposing perspective as the one doing the bothering. Except she'd never felt like it was a bother when he'd sought her out and, secretly, she'd always reveled in Desmond's attention.

Desmond: *Is everything okay?*

McKenna: *Peachy. Why do you ask?*

Desmond: *It's midnight.*

McKenna: *Yes, I noticed that. I was worried about you.*

She swore and tried to click on the message to recall it so she could correct that to *Conner* but he was already typing.

Desmond: *Don't do this. The adjustment is hard enough.*

She blinked. Don't do what? Be concerned? Talk to him via the chat tool he'd installed? The list of things he might be asking her to refrain from doing was long, but the better question was why he'd even say something like that.

McKenna: *What adjusting do you have to do? I'm the one in a new place.*

Desmond: *That was your choice. I have plenty to adjust to. I haven't ever been a father by myself. I miss you.*

Oh, God. She missed him, too. More than she could stand sometimes. Before she could react to that—unfreeze her fingers, breathe, *something*—he sent another message.

Desmond: *I can't do this with you.*

And then his status immediately flipped to offline. Stunned, she stared at the screen, her mind racing through that pseudo conversation, trying to pinpoint how she'd upset him. And it was very clear that she was indeed the problem. *I can't do this with you* sat there as a silent accusation, as cryptic as his initial unpunctuated and uncapitalized "hi."

Desmond missed her. It was right there in black surrounded by a blue bubble. She couldn't stop staring at it as she internalized that he might have a much bigger emotional stake in their relationship than she'd supposed. And if that was true, their conversation was far from over.

Oh, God. He missed her. He wasn't sleeping.

Everything but Desmond drained away.

She'd made a huge mistake.

Medical school could wait. Her family couldn't.

She yanked out her phone and texted him. Can't do what?

Let's see how you deal with that, Desmond H. Pierce. She'd entered him into an unbreakable social contract that required him to communicate back.

Except he didn't.

McKenna texted him again. Talk to me.

Thirty minutes later he hadn't complied. Furious with herself for caring whether or not she'd made a choice without all the facts, she stalked to the car and did the one thing she'd sworn never to do. She drove to Desmond's house. Ridiculous, stupid plan. But the panicky feeling in her stomach wouldn't stop and her brain kept turning over the fact that she hadn't really asked Desmond what her choices were when it came to what he was proposing.

The gate admitted her car without any trouble, a telling sign since it was automated to scan the license plate. Desmond had added her Honda to the list. Why?

At the front door she sent another text message: I'm outside. Come tell me to go away. She was going to get him to talk to her one way or another.

The front door cracked open less than thirty seconds later. Light spilled from the foyer, casting the man who'd opened it in shadow.

"It's late," Desmond rumbled into the darkness. "What are you doing here?"

His voice washed over her and her knees went a little weak. What *was* she doing here? She'd left this house because she hadn't seen any way to stay that wouldn't make her insane. Apparently sanity wasn't the goal because here she was again, begging for this man to talk to her, to change the tide, to force her to choose happiness instead of duty.

"Do you know what my favorite quality of yours is?" she asked instead of answering his question. Mostly because she didn't know how to answer it. Her mind was a riot of illogical, fragmented thoughts.

He sighed. "I must not have been clear. I don't want to talk to you. You made your choice to walk away. But I can make a choice to not let you back into my life."

Yes. She'd walked away. Toward a medical degree, which had long been her goal, but she'd also left something precious behind.

"That's my favorite quality of yours." She poked him in the chest because she couldn't stand not touching him a second longer. "You tell me exactly what's on your mind. Except when you don't. And that's what got me into the car, Desmond. Our conversation wasn't finished."

"Yes, it was, McKenna. There's nothing left to say."

The pain lacing his voice nearly stole her breath. She'd *hurt* him. *That* was why he kept shutting her down. While she'd been determined to get his attention strictly for her own peace of mind, he was trying to push her off because she'd hurt him.

She'd had no idea he cared that much.

What else didn't she know?

"I beg to differ," she countered softly and curled her hand around the open neckline of his button-down, holding tight and totally unsure if it was to keep him from fleeing or to keep her from dissolving into a little puddle at his feet. He wasn't dressed for bed, which might be the most telling of all. "I think there's a lot left to say. Like why you let me leave."

"Why I *let* you leave?" His short laugh raked through her. "I don't recall being given the choice. You demanded all the choices and then made your decision. What else could you possibly expect me to say other than I simply stepped out of your way."

It wasn't a question. It was a statement. A conviction. He'd done exactly as she'd told him to. Instead of having a conversation, she'd slung her own need for control around, forcing him to step back. What else might he have said if she'd shut her mouth?

She stared at him as he let her glimpse the anguish her choices had caused. Or maybe the things he felt were too strong to keep inside. "I expect you to tell me I'm selfish and I messed up. That I walked away from my family because of stupid pride and a need to do things my own way. As a result, I lost the two most important things that ever happened to me."

"That's not true." His gaze turned indignant as he argued with her. "Medical school was always important. You're incredibly intelligent, personable. Driven. You'll make an excellent doctor."

That curled up in her chest in tight, warm ball. "That's the nicest thing anyone's ever said to me."

He shrugged. "That's why I stepped out of the way and smoothed your path. I owed it to you, as you pointed out time and time again. I let you leave because it was never my right to force you to stay."

Her heart cracked open, spilling out love and pain and adoration and regret. He really did get it, displaying a wealth of understanding and willingness to change, which she'd failed to value. She did now.

"You couldn't have forced me to stay. Instead you set me free. That one act allowed me the time and distance to see where I wanted to land. It's here. With you. And

Conner. I made a mistake." Desperate to make him understand, she gripped his shirt tighter. "Please tell me it's not too late to pick up the pieces of our marriage."

He shook his head. "It's too late, McKenna. I can't let you go again."

"But that's not what I'm asking you to do," she whispered. "I'm not going anywhere. I choose to stay this time."

The short, simple phrase bled through Desmond's chest, slicing open new wounds as it burrowed toward his heart seeking asylum. "You can't say things like that."

Not now. Not after he'd already reconciled that his family had been torn apart. He'd cataloged all the emotion, analyzed everything that had gone wrong and arrived at the conclusion that he wasn't cut out for this madness.

Some people were natural artists, others were gifted musicians. Desmond's talent was trusting a woman with life-altering power. And when the woman exercised that power, she dug big, gaping holes in his soul that would never be filled. Loneliness and isolation plagued him and he lacked the ability to resolve either.

"Why?" she asked. "Is the invitation to stay rescinded? I didn't hear a time limit attached."

"Please don't do this." It was too much for him to breathe her in and let his senses get that one long taste of her. "You're enrolled in medical school. The die is cast."

"Then why haven't you filed for the divorce yet?" she countered quietly.

That nearly broke him. She wanted truth?

"Because you're still my wife, no matter what," he admitted.

Her expression veered wildly between extremes and finally settled on tenderness. "Yes. I am. And I want a chance to see what that looks like when we both give up our need for control."

"I've already done that once, McKenna. Never again." Harsh. Although still just the plain truth. If nothing else, he'd learned that life did not go as planned simply because he willed it to be so, but he could certainly curtail the damage by never opening himself up again. He'd spent years hiding, which suited him fine. Nothing had changed.

"I hurt you." At his curt nod, both of her hands slid up his arms to squeeze his shoulders and her touch almost knocked his composure away like a cat amused by a ball of yarn. "I'm sorry. I didn't honor how difficult that was for you, to give me the choice to leave. I made the wrong decision because I couldn't see myself as anything other than a doctor. I'm not good at failing and I didn't handle the dynamic between us well."

"What dynamic?" he couldn't help but ask and then wished to bite off his tongue. He might as well come out and ask if she'd developed feelings for him that she'd yet to share. Pathetic. Hadn't he learned his lesson? Women were treacherous.

"The one where I wanted to stay but couldn't see how that would work."

Her warm hands hadn't moved from his shoulders and he leaned into her touch, craving it and cursing himself for the craving at the same time. But he'd long ceased looking for a way to resist her because that was the very definition of insanity—doing the same thing over and over again without better results. Resisting her was impossible.

"The one where I fell into your world and couldn't

break free," she whispered. "You opened your door and eventually your body, your mind, your heart, and I... loved all of it. Especially your mind."

"Again, very short list of people in that category," he countered, not at all shocked that the gruff note in his voice perfectly matched the insurrection of emotion exploding through his chest. "If you wanted to stay, why didn't you?"

"I'm selfish and stubborn, or didn't you get the memo?" she asked wryly, and he refused to smile, though it was clear she'd meant for him to.

"You're the least selfish person I know. Everything you've done since I've met you has been for someone else. You'll be a great doctor," he repeated because the point couldn't be made clearly enough. He couldn't stand the thought of her resenting him for standing in her way. "You're also an amazing mother and the only wife I could imagine letting into my world."

Her eyelids fluttered closed as she processed that and, when she opened them, the clearest sense of hope radiated from her eyes. "You've always seen me as more than I do. I didn't believe in myself nearly as much as you did. I never thought I could be more than a doctor. It was too hard to concentrate when I had Conner and you right down the hall."

That was definitely something they had in common. He'd been unable to focus on anything other than her since that first moment she'd invaded his workshop without invitation, barging into his consciousness without fear, and he'd never been able to let her go in all the days since.

Even this one. Case in point. They were having a conversation at one in the morning instead of sleeping. Nothing worked to exorcise her from his mind, her scent from his head and the ghost of her in his bed.

"Then I have to ask. Did it get easier when you left?" If it had, he'd move in an instant to somewhere he could concentrate without her invading his everything.

"No." She smiled and it grabbed hold of his lungs, heart—hell, all of his internal organs at once. "I'm afraid it only got worse. So the problem is that I can't be a doctor without you. I can't be a mother without Conner. So here I am. Now what?"

Oh, no. She wasn't throwing that ball back in his court. "That's not my choice. It can't be."

"Then that makes it mine by default. So you're stuck with me," she informed him loftily. "The only thing is that you have to forgive me for wasting your tuition money. It's too late in the semester to get a refund."

"You're quitting school?" Incredulous, he stared at her. "You can't do that. *Why* would you do that? That's the worst possible choice you could make."

"Please, Desmond. Don't lock yourself away from me. I'm begging you for another chance." She shook him fiercely as if trying to knock that chance loose by sheer force. "Are you listening to what I'm saying? I'm not leaving again. I can't. I love you too much."

So many wondrous emotions radiated from her skin and burrowed under his, winnowing toward his soul too fast for him to catch it all or block it somehow. Too late. She swept away the shadows that had crawled inside him since she'd left.

"You shouldn't," he countered as his heart knit back together so fast he went light-headed. "I'm difficult to love—"

"Shut up. Stop saying stuff like that. What's difficult is when I try to stop loving you." She laughed and one tear slipped down her face as she shared what was inside her. "I don't know how to be in love. It's scary. It has no way for me to control it. Instead of telling you this, I left."

"To be a doctor. You had a dream that I wasn't a part of. I respected that even as it tore me apart."

"I know." Her head bowed for a brief moment. "That's what finally broke me, I think. That you were willing to sacrifice for me in spite of everything."

"I still am," he admitted gruffly. "It's the least I can do for what you sacrificed to give me Conner. Please don't give up medical school."

"It's okay, I have something better. A family."

That was the part that broke *him*. He swept her into his embrace and clung, scarcely able to believe he was holding her again.

"I love you," he murmured, unable to stop the flow of words. "So much. Too much to let you make such an irrevocable choice. There's absolutely no reason you can't keep going to school. I'll move to the house near campus. Tomorrow. Conner and I will take care of you while you become a doctor."

"You'd do that?" His shoulder muffled her broken whisper but he heard the question inside the question regardless.

"Of course I would. I'm already the nanny. Why not the househusband? I would live in a shack on the side of the road if that's what you wanted. As long as you were in it." He tipped up her chin to lay his lips on hers in what was only the first of many kisses to come. "This is just a house where I build things. If I have a family, I've already built the most important creation of my life. Anything else is just icing on the cake."

She smiled through her tears. "That sounds like an easy choice then."

"None of this is supposed to be hard. I told you, all you have to do is lie there and command me to do your will."

"I don't understand why you would do all of this for me."

Because to her he wasn't a beast. He wasn't the weird, awkward kid no one wanted to sit by. She'd chosen *him*. That was awe inspiring. And probably the only thing that could have enticed him out of his reclusive fortress designed to keep out the world.

But it turned out he didn't have to. McKenna had brought the world to him.

"Also not hard. I love you and you gave me Conner. The real question is what I could possibly do to repay you for the miracle of our son. I still don't know. But I'm going to spend a very long time trying to answer that. If you'll allow me to rip up the divorce papers."

She nodded furiously. "I'd like to burn them. In the fireplace. So I know for sure they're gone forever."

"Done. Except you'll have to wait until morning because I plan to be very busy between now and then." He couldn't stand to let her go as he led her toward the stairs and the bedroom upstairs that had been cold and empty without her.

"Oh, what did you have in mind?" she asked saucily with an intrigued expression that wasn't difficult to interpret. She was game for whatever he could envision, which excited him to no end. He had a great imagination.

"Sleep," he said with a laugh. "I haven't done that since you left and I'm looking forward to many nights of recovery."

She scowled without any real heat. "Sleep? I drove all the way from Portland to tell you my life is meaningless without you and you want to go to bed to *sleep*?"

"Maybe in a little while. I have some lost time to make up for first." And then he claimed his wife's lips in a kiss that was the second miracle he'd experienced in his life. He couldn't wait to find out what the next one would be.

Epilogue

McKenna swept Conner up for a hug, kissing him soundly on the cheek, but the precocious, dark-haired three-year-old was having none of that. He squirmed out of his mother's grip and ran off to play with Mark Hudson's daughter, the only other little person at the university's graduation ceremony.

Desmond smiled at his wife as she paused to exchange hugs with Mark's wife, Roberta. They'd socialized with the couple occasionally as Mark and McKenna worked through residency, but more often than not, Roberta and Desmond traded babysitting duty to give the other household a break during the grueling three years of medical school their respective spouses had endured.

It was over now. They'd both graduated with honors and earned their medical degrees.

"Dr. Pierce," Des murmured in his wife's ear as she paused at the reception table for a bottle of water. Happiness radiated from her, nearly dripping from her skin. "I've been waiting a long time to call you that."

She grinned and leaned into his embrace, which worked for him because that was where he wanted her. Always.

"Only because you're tired of being the only Dr. Pierce in our house."

Home. Not a house. They lived in a home, barely twelve hundred square feet worth, but he loved it. Had watched Conner take his first steps in the living room. Kissed McKenna at the dining room table as she'd applied for her second year of medical school, her residency, her name change.

"Perhaps," he conceded with a nod.

But more to the point, they'd agreed that once she'd earned her diploma, they'd throw caution to the wind and see what happened when McKenna stopped taking her birth control pills. For three years he'd been patient, letting her focus on medical school as promised.

She'd graduated. Tonight was his turn.

"Come with me, Dr. Pierce," he growled as the festivities wound down. "The Hudsons are taking Conner home with them for the night. You're all mine."

"Why, Dr. Pierce, whatever do you have in mind?" McKenna shifted her long dark hair off one shoulder as she contemplated him with a saucy smile. "A little graduation party for two?"

"Yes."

She laughed and the clear sound trilled through him. "Glad I'm not a big fan of suspense. You're as transparent as glass."

Still her favorite quality of his, as she told him often. Good thing. Saved him a lot of trouble explaining things.

"Then it should be no surprise what I've got planned. Kiss your son and let's go."

He waited impatiently as she gave Roberta a few instructions, including the one about making sure Conner had his elephant, Peter, to sleep with. And then, finally, he got her snuggled into his embrace for the five-minute walk to their little clapboard house that had not one robotic humanoid inside its walls.

The remote mansion on the river sat untouched, a monument to the man he'd once been and never would be again. But he couldn't bear to sell it because it was still the place where he'd fallen in love with his wife, where he'd first made love to her. One day, Conner might want to live there and have access to all the luxuries. But for now, all they needed was each other.

Once she cleared the door, McKenna turned in his arms, trapping him against the wood. There was no place on earth he'd rather be. His arms were full of light, desire, happiness. So many emotions raced through her, he could hardly sense one before another took over.

"Tonight's the night," he told her. "If this isn't what you want, you should tell me now."

He really didn't have to clarify. But it was always nice to hear her voice.

"Which part?" she murmured against his throat as she nibbled his skin. "Where I command you to strip me naked and have your wicked way with me?"

"The part where I get you pregnant," he corrected, his voice so rough with need it was a wonder she understood him. "Finally."

But then, she'd never had a problem understanding him.

"I've been waiting three long years for this, Des." She smiled, her hands busy unbuckling his belt. "I want to conceive your baby and, alongside you, watch it grow in my tummy. I want a brother or sister for Conner. A legacy that has everything to do with love."

That sounded perfect to Desmond. "Then come here and let me love you."

He swept his wife into his arms and took her to bed where the only thing that stood between them was skin. He did his best to savor each moment, to pay attention to the subtle cues so he could pinpoint the exact moment of conception. But in the end there was too much going on and he let the sheer pleasure of her reign supreme because what else mattered?

"You know it might take more than one try to conceive," she murmured later as they lay content in each other's arms.

"I'm nothing if not ready, willing and able to try as many times as I need to."

Smiling so wide it hurt his face, he stroked her arm. A baby would be amazing. A fantastic addition to the family he'd built, that they continued to build every day. McKenna had drawn him out from behind his curtain into the real world. And they had lots of opportunities to perfect the art of baby making. They should probably start over right now.

* * * * *

MILLS & BOON®
Hardback – May 2017

ROMANCE

The Sheikh's Bought Wife	Sharon Kendrick
The Innocent's Shameful Secret	Sara Craven
The Magnate's Tempestuous Marriage	Miranda Lee
The Forced Bride of Alazar	Kate Hewitt
Bound by the Sultan's Baby	Carol Marinelli
Blackmailed Down the Aisle	Louise Fuller
Di Marcello's Secret Son	Rachael Thomas
The Italian's Vengeful Seduction	Bella Frances
Conveniently Wed to the Greek	Kandy Shepherd
His Shy Cinderella	Kate Hardy
Falling for the Rebel Princess	Ellie Darkins
Claimed by the Wealthy Magnate	Nina Milne
Mummy, Nurse...Duchess?	Kate Hardy
Falling for the Foster Mum	Karin Baine
The Doctor and the Princess	Scarlet Wilson
Miracle for the Neurosurgeon	Lynne Marshall
English Rose for the Sicilian Doc	Annie Claydon
Engaged to the Doctor Sheikh	Meredith Webber
The Marriage Contract	Kat Cantrell
Triplets for the Texan	Janice Maynard

MILLS & BOON®
Large Print – May 2017

ROMANCE

A Deal for the Di Sione Ring	Jennifer Hayward
The Italian's Pregnant Virgin	Maisey Yates
A Dangerous Taste of Passion	Anne Mather
Bought to Carry His Heir	Jane Porter
Married for the Greek's Convenience	Michelle Smart
Bound by His Desert Diamond	Andie Brock
A Child Claimed by Gold	Rachael Thomas
Her New Year Baby Secret	Jessica Gilmore
Slow Dance with the Best Man	Sophie Pembroke
The Prince's Convenient Proposal	Barbara Hannay
The Tycoon's Reluctant Cinderella	Therese Beharrie

HISTORICAL

The Wedding Game	Christine Merrill
Secrets of the Marriage Bed	Ann Lethbridge
Compromising the Duke's Daughter	Mary Brendan
In Bed with the Viking Warrior	Harper St. George
Married to Her Enemy	Jenni Fletcher

MEDICAL

The Nurse's Christmas Gift	Tina Beckett
The Midwife's Pregnancy Miracle	Kate Hardy
Their First Family Christmas	Alison Roberts
The Nightshift Before Christmas	Annie O'Neil
It Started at Christmas...	Janice Lynn
Unwrapped by the Duke	Amy Ruttan

MILLS & BOON®
Hardback – June 2017

ROMANCE

Sold for the Greek's Heir	Lynne Graham
The Prince's Captive Virgin	Maisey Yates
The Secret Sanchez Heir	Cathy Williams
The Prince's Nine-Month Scandal	Caitlin Crews
Her Sinful Secret	Jane Porter
The Drakon Baby Bargain	Tara Pammi
Xenakis's Convenient Bride	Dani Collins
The Greek's Pleasurable Revenge	Andie Brock
Her Pregnancy Bombshell	Liz Fielding
Married for His Secret Heir	Jennifer Faye
Behind the Billionaire's Guarded Heart	Leah Ashton
A Marriage Worth Saving	Therese Beharrie
Healing the Sheikh's Heart	Annie O'Neil
A Life-Saving Reunion	Alison Roberts
The Surgeon's Cinderella	Susan Carlisle
Saved by Doctor Dreamy	Dianne Drake
Pregnant with the Boss's Baby	Sue MacKay
Reunited with His Runaway Doc	Lucy Clark
His Accidental Heir	Joanne Rock
A Texas-Sized Secret	Maureen Child

MILLS & BOON®
Large Print – June 2017

ROMANCE

The Last Di Sione Claims His Prize	Maisey Yates
Bought to Wear the Billionaire's Ring	Cathy Williams
The Desert King's Blackmailed Bride	Lynne Graham
Bride by Royal Decree	Caitlin Crews
The Consequence of His Vengeance	Jennie Lucas
The Sheikh's Secret Son	Maggie Cox
Acquired by Her Greek Boss	Chantelle Shaw
The Sheikh's Convenient Princess	Liz Fielding
The Unforgettable Spanish Tycoon	Christy McKellen
The Billionaire of Coral Bay	Nikki Logan
Her First-Date Honeymoon	Katrina Cudmore

HISTORICAL

The Harlot and the Sheikh	Marguerite Kaye
The Duke's Secret Heir	Sarah Mallory
Miss Bradshaw's Bought Betrothal	Virginia Heath
Sold to the Viking Warrior	Michelle Styles
A Marriage of Rogues	Margaret Moore

MEDICAL

White Christmas for the Single Mum	Susanne Hampton
A Royal Baby for Christmas	Scarlet Wilson
Playboy on Her Christmas List	Carol Marinelli
The Army Doc's Baby Bombshell	Sue MacKay
The Doctor's Sleigh Bell Proposal	Susan Carlisle
Christmas with the Single Dad	Louisa Heaton

MILLS & BOON®

Why shop at millsandboon.co.uk?

Each year, thousands of romance readers find their perfect read at millsandboon.co.uk. That's because we're passionate about bringing you the very best romantic fiction. Here are some of the advantages of shopping at www.millsandboon.co.uk:

* **Get new books first**—you'll be able to buy your favourite books one month before they hit the shops

* **Get exclusive discounts**—you'll also be able to buy our specially created monthly collections, with up to 50% off the RRP

* **Find your favourite authors**—latest news, interviews and new releases for all your favourite authors and series on our website, plus ideas for what to try next

* **Join in**—once you've bought your favourite books, don't forget to register with us to rate, review and join in the discussions

Visit **www.millsandboon.co.uk**
for all this and more today!